LIFE CRAFTER DEATH

A Knitorious Murder Mystery

REAGAN DAVIS

COPYRIGHT

FOREWORD

Dear Reader,

Despite several layers of editing and proofreading, occasionally a typo or grammar mistake is so stubborn that it manages to thwart my editing efforts and camouflage itself amongst the words in the book.

If you encounter one of these obstinate typos or errors in this book, please let me know by contacting me at Hello@ReaganDavis.com.

Hopefully, together we can exterminate the annoying pests.

Thank you!

Reagan Davis

CONTENTS

CHAPTER 1

FRIDAY, October 1st

We live ten hours apart, but I see my sister, Emmy, almost every day. Millions of people see her every day. She co-hosts the popular morning show, *Hello, today!*

"Good girl, Soph," I say as the corgi brushes past my legs and through the open door.

She propels herself off the deck and onto the frost-covered lawn, triggering the motion detector which illuminates the pre-dawn backyard with harsh, artificial light.

While Sophie does her business and conducts her first perimeter check of the day, I fix her breakfast, drop a pumpkin spice coffee pod in the coffeemaker, and turn on the TV to catch my daily glimpse of my sister.

The TV comes to life, permeating the family room and kitchen with *Hello, today!*'s snappy theme music. I retrieve my mug from the coffeemaker and savour the first glorious sip of soul-satisfying caffeine while watching the title sequence. Cast and crew member names fade in and out as my sister zooms across the TV screen, riding a Segway through the studio. Then the camera cuts to footage of her and her co-host cooking with a celebrity chef. Then another cut to footage of Emmy drinking from an oversized *Hello, today!* mug while someone touches up her hair and makeup. She and the makeup artist burst into laughter.

Hello, today! is a typical infotainment morning show. Two co-hosts and their colleagues broadcast live, cycling between news, traffic, weather, and sports updates, interspersed with lifestyle and human interest segments.

It's early, and the world is still dark and quiet, but I'm wide awake. As a reluctant morning person, I'm wired to wake up early. I envy people whose internal clocks let them sleep past dawn, but I'm not one of them. This time of year, when the days are shorter, I'm up and at 'em before the sun.

Sophie scratches at the back door, and I look away from the TV to let her in. Sophie shakes off the early morning chill, buries her face in her food dish, and devours her breakfast with enthusiasm.

"...is filling in for Miranda Monroe, who's under the weather. Feel better, Miranda!"

I spin and look at the TV when Rich Kendall—pronounced Rich Ken-doll—announces that my sister isn't at work today. Apparently, she's sick.

Miranda Monroe is my sister's given name and the name she uses professionally. Our names are almost identical, not our parents' most creative moment. They

2

named me Megan Elizabeth Monroe, and named my sister, Miranda Elizabeth Monroe.

According to our father, when Emmy was born, sixteen-month-old me had yet to develop the necessary verbal skills to pronounce Miranda. My garbled attempt to say my baby sister's name sounded like Emmy, so that's what everyone called her. It stuck. Friends and family still call her Emmy. Despite three marriages, and three name changes, Emmy has always used her maiden name on television.

I whip my phone out of my housecoat pocket and check my text messages. Emmy always texts me when she misses work. Always. No text. I type a quick message.

Me: Are you OK? Rich said you're sick.

I hit send and stare at the screen, waiting for the three dots to appear that show my sister is typing a reply. We always reply to each other's texts right away. No dots. Hmmm.

"Good morning, Mrs. Sloane!" Eric says, shutting the front door behind him.

"Umm… we're not married yet," I remind him with a grin.

"I know. I'm practicing. I like the way it sounds."

Eric Sloane is my fiancé and chief of the Harmony Lake Police Department.

I scrunch my nose at his muskiness when he kisses me good morning.

His skin glistens and his short, dark hair is damp with sweat. He just finished a run. I can't imagine running this early—scratch that—I can't imagine

3

running. Eric possesses a terrifying and impressive amount of self-discipline.

"Hug?" he teases, his open arms drawing attention to the sweat-soaked shirt clinging to his fat-free, well-muscled torso.

"After you have a shower," I reply, taking a step backward, just in case he's serious.

He squats to greet Sophie, who's tippy-tapping her paws on the floor at his feet, waiting for him to notice her.

"Where's Emmy?" Eric lifts his chin toward the TV, where Emmy's usual spot on the *Hello, today!* sofa is occupied by the person who provides weather updates.

"Rich said she's sick."

I check my phone again, in case my sister replied to my text, and I missed the notification.

"Is she OK?" Eric asks, squeezing his eyebrows together.

"I don't know," I reply, shaking my head. "She hasn't answered my text."

"I'm sure she's fine," Eric assures me, sensing my concern. "It's probably just a cold or something. She probably went back to bed."

"Probably," I agree.

My phone dings.

"See," Eric says, "that's her. Telling you she's fine."

I nod in acknowledgement and unlock my phone. It's a text, but not from Emmy. It's from my best friend, April.

"April," I tell Eric with a sigh. "She's asking if Emmy is OK because she's not on *Hello, today!*"

"How's their trip?" Eric asks.

April and her wife are out of town for a family wedding. They won't be back until next Friday. This is the longest April and her wife have ever left their bakery. April's wife is a talented pastry chef and together they own Artsy Tartsy, Harmony Lake's local bakery. While they're away, their pastry-chef friend is working at the bakery, staying at their house, and taking care of their cats.

"They're having a great time," I reply to Eric's question. "It helps that Marla is working at the bakery every day and texting them regular, reassuring updates."

Marla is one of my part-time employees. While April and Tamara are away, she's splitting her part-time hours between my yarn store, Knitorious, and Artsy Tartsy.

"Do you need me to help at the store today?" Eric offers.

Eric isn't working today. He's using some time off the department owes him for overtime he's worked.

"No, thanks," I reply. "You should enjoy your day off, not spend it shelving yarn and cashing out customers."

"I enjoy hanging out at Knitorious." He winks. "I have a huge crush on the owner. I can't stay away from her." With a glint of playful mischief in his brown eyes, Eric cocks one eyebrow and takes a step toward me. "Can you go in late? We could have breakfast together or something."

A familiar twinge of temptation tugs at me from

deep inside, but my overdeveloped sense of responsi-
bility overrides my desire to play hooky.

"I can't," I say, wishing I could. "We're short-staffed
with Marla helping at the bakery.

"There are plenty of odd jobs to keep me busy at
home today," Eric says with a sigh. "But if you want to
come home for lunch…" he winks.

"I'll do my best," I say. "And I'll give Sophie the day
off to keep you company."

Sophie's ears perk up when she hears her name. She
comes to work with me every day, but she'll be happy
to stay home with Eric.

"I'M SURE EMMY IS FINE," Connie insists, tucking her
sleek silver bob behind her ear. "She's probably asleep,
and she'll text you when she wakes up."

Connie is my other part-time employee. She was the
original owner of Knitorious. I worked for her part time
until she retired, then I took over the store. Connie and I
are more than colleagues, we're family. Chosen family.
Connie and I met when I moved to Harmony Lake
almost twenty years ago. I was only twenty-one years
old, new in town, lonely, and overwhelmed. My
husband was an ambitious young lawyer who spent
most of his time at his office in the city. My daughter,
Hannah, was a baby and I was a new, anxious mother.
To top it off, my own mother had recently passed away
unexpectedly. I was overwhelmed. To cope, I channeled
my energy into knitting while Hannah slept. One day,

realizing I'd knitted through my yarn stash, I pushed Hannah's stroller into Knitorious and met Connie. She took us under her wing and filled the mother and grandmother-shaped holes in our hearts.

"I'd feel better if I knew for sure," I respond.

"Who's Emmy?" Tina asks from a sofa in the cozy sitting area, her eyes laser-focused on the stitch she's knitting.

Tina Duran is new to Harmony Lake. She moved here a few months ago, looking for a fresh start after her divorce. She works at one of the mountain resorts. Tina's also a novice knitter, and Connie has been guiding and encouraging her on her knitting journey.

"Emmy is my sister," I reply. "She hasn't returned my text, which is out of character for her."

I don't explain that Emmy is Miranda Monroe, the popular television morning show host.

Today, Tina's learning how to knit in the round by making Knitted Knockers. Every October, in honour of Breast Cancer Awareness Month, the Harmony Lake Charity Knitting Guild makes and donates Knitted Knockers. These are handmade breast prostheses for women who have undergone mastectomies or other breast procedures.

"I'm sure you'll hear from her," Tina says.

I'm about to agree with Tina when my phone dings.

"Maybe it's Emmy!" Connie suggests optimistically, reaching for my phone on the counter and handing it to me. "She probably went back to bed and just woke up."

I unlock my phone and look at the screen with a heavy sigh.

"It's April." I exhale and place the phone on the coffee table in front of me. "She sent me a funny video of a cat using dog treats to get a German Shepherd to do tricks." I smile at Connie. "If Emmy hasn't texted me by this afternoon, I'll phone her."

Tina places her knitting in her lap. "Maybe her phone died or something." She shrugs and places her knitting in her backpack, then slings her backpack over one shoulder, and stands up. "I have to go to work."

I suspect Tina is around my age, forty-one, or in her late thirties, but it's hard to tell, and it would be rude to ask. Her style of dress and the way she talks makes her seem younger, but Tina refers to movies, and music that I grew up with, which makes me think she looks younger than her actual age. Her dark hair shows no signs of grey, her brown eyes are bright, and her complexion is smooth and ageless. She has a hint of an accent that's difficult to place, but lovely to listen to. She says her accent is a combination of all the places she's lived. She was born in Brazil, but went to university in Europe. Then, after she got married, she moved around the US and Canada for her husband's job.

"I hope you hear from your sister," Tina says with a smile.

Connie and I wish her a good day, and she leaves.

"Mothballs!" Connie mutters her version of an expletive.

"What's wrong?"

"Tina left her jacket," Connie replies, pointing to the jacket draped over the back of the sofa. "That girl always leaves something behind," Connie muses, picking up the jacket and smoothing it over her arm. "I'll hang it up in the backroom."

"I'll send her a text so she knows where she left it," I offer.

According to my phone, it's almost lunchtime. I'll wait one more hour, then if I still haven't heard from Emmy, I'll phone her.

I try to focus on texting Tina, but I can't quiet the voice inside my head. It's a constant whisper warning me the reason I haven't heard from Emmy is because something is wrong. Very wrong.

CHAPTER 2

CONNIE IS on her lunch break, and I'm washing the floor-to-ceiling display windows to distract myself from worrying about Emmy.

I flinch when the door swings open and slams against the wall with enough force to shake the yarn shelves and cause the bell to make a startling, loud crash.

"Emmy?" I blink and do a double take when my sister swoops into the store. "What are you doing here? Are you OK?" I ask, shocked to see her but relieved that she appears healthy and unharmed.

"It's over!" Emmy announces, throwing her hands into the air. "Phone Adam. I need him to represent me in the divorce!" she demands, sniffling. "Again," she adds under her breath.

Adam Martel is my ex-husband. He's also Harmony Lake's resident lawyer and our town's mayor. He represented Emmy in her first two divorces.

"What happened?" I ask, stepping out of the display window.

I close the door, making sure Emmy's dramatic entrance didn't damage it or the wall.

"Armando wants to destroy my career," she announces. "The network asked us to be contestants on the next season of *Perfect Match*. The big wigs think it will draw *Hello, today!* viewers to *Perfect Match*, and draw *Perfect Match* viewers to *Hello, today!*" She breaks into sobs. "Armando refused! Can you believe that, Sis? This is a huge career opportunity for me. Why does he hate me?" Emmy bursts into tears and sobs into a wadded-up tissue clenched in her fist.

I envelop my sister in a hug, and she collapses into my arms.

Armando Garcia is Emmy's husband. He's a professional soccer player. They've been married for three years, but I don't know Armando very well because his hectic schedule keeps him on the road most of the year. He's rarely available to accompany my sister when she visits Harmony Lake, and whenever I visit her, he's away playing soccer.

Perfect Match is a reality television show where eight B-list celebrity couples live in the *Perfect Match* house, sequestered from the outside world. Each week they face a challenge designed to test the strength of their relationship. A challenge could be something like one person being tempted by an attractive distraction, someone's former flame showing up, dealing with rumours about each other, or one person being encouraged by their housemates to keep a secret from their partner. Drama, strategic alliances, and secret relationships ensue. Each week, the home audience votes online to determine which couple failed the weekly challenge. Then, at the start of the next episode, the host reveals last week's disgraced couple and evicts them from the *Perfect Match* house. This continues until one couple remains; the last couple wins the title of *Perfect Match* and gets to return for the tournament of champions called *Perfect Match: Playing With Fire*. I don't watch the show. The concept doesn't appeal to me. Relationships are hard enough without competing to prove your love for each other in front of a prime-time audience. I understand why Armando would rather not take part.

"Did Armando say why?" I ask, leading Emmy to the cozy sitting area and helping her into an overstuffed chair.

"He says filming will interfere with soccer," Emmy snorts, rolling her eyes. "Also, *Brad*,"—Emmy sneers with contempt when she says his name—"told him appearing on the show would *devalue the Armando Garcia brand*. Whatever that means." She blows her nose. "Brad hates me!"

Brad Hendricks is Armando's agent. He negotiates Armando's sponsorship deals, media appearances, and such.

"I'm sure Brad doesn't hate you," I reassure her, having no actual insight into Brad's feelings about my sister.

"He's always hated me, and this is another way for him to sabotage my marriage." She breaks into a fresh fit of sobs. "Armando doesn't see it. He thinks Brad is his friend. If Armando had listened to me and found a new agent when we got married, I wouldn't be here right now."

"Maybe Armando doesn't want to spend the little time you have together filming a reality TV show," I suggest, trying to temper her extreme perspective while I hand her a box of tissues.

It's amazing how little time my sister and her husband spend together. Between training camp, preseason games, regular season games, postseason games, and public appearances, Armando travels over two hundred days each year. Emmy's Monday-to-Friday job on *Hello, today!* keeps her anchored to their hometown, and she devotes much of her time off to promotional appearances for worthy causes and for the network.

The bell above the door jingles—gentler this time—and Sophie appears at our feet, wagging her Corgi tail and panting. Torn between visiting me or Emmy first, Emmy wins and Sophie places her front paws on her knees.

"Hey, Soph," Emmy whispers, scratching Sophie between the ears.

"Emmy! This is a pleasant surprise," Eric says, then he looks at me. "See! I told you she was OK." He smiles at Emmy, and she looks up at him with her watery eyes and quivering chin. He looks at me again. "She's not OK, is she?"

I shake my head.

Eric places a to-go cup from Latte Da on the counter. A chocolate caramel latte, my current favourite specialty coffee from their fall menu. The chocolaty coffee aroma makes my mouth water from ten feet away.

"It's nice to see you, Eric," Emmy says, standing up and giving him a hug. "Megan, I'll be right back. I need to freshen up."

"Of course," I say, rubbing her back reassuringly. "Take your time."

Emmy tosses her bag over her shoulder and heads toward the backroom with Sophie guiding the way.

"What's going on?" Eric whispers.

"Domestic quarrel," I whisper in reply.

He nods and his mouth forms a tiny o.

"I told Adam I'd meet him for a round of golf later," Eric explains. "But I'll cancel if you need me."

Yes, my fiancé and my ex-husband are friends. Good friends. They golf and watch sports together. It was weird at first, but we're all used to it now. Adam and I might be divorced, but we're still family and have forged a strong friendship from the wreckage of our marriage. We're determined to keep our family intact for the sake of our daughter, and Eric supports that.

"Thank you, honey, but go. This could be your last round of the year," I say, referring to the unseasonable, summer-like weather we've enjoyed this week.

"Are you sure?" Eric looks unconvinced.

"Positive." I stand on my tippy toes and give him a kiss. Eric is almost a foot taller than me, so even when I wear heels, kissing requires some stretching on my part and some stooping on his. "Connie will be back from lunch soon, and Emmy's exhausted, so I'll probably send her home to rest. If you're golfing, the house will be quiet for her."

Persuaded to keep his golf date, Eric kisses my forehead, reminds me to call him if I need anything, and leaves. On his way out, he holds the door open for Tina as she rushes into Knitorious, breathless and flushed as if she ran here.

"Hey, Tina," I greet her with a smile. "You seem like you're in a hurry."

"Kind of." Tina nods and catches her breath. "I'm on my break and came to pick up my jacket."

"Right," I say, remembering Connie saying something about hanging Tina's jacket in the backroom. "Connie put it in the back. I'll get for you."

Tina's jacket isn't hanging on the coat rack by the back door, and at first glance, it's not in the closet. I turn on the closet light and slide the hangers over one by one.

"Aha! Found you!" I inform the jacket with a smug sense of victory when I find it squashed between two parkas that belong to the tenants who live in the apartment above the store.

"Got it," I announce, striding from the backroom to the front of the store.

Tina can't hear me because she's mesmerized by Emmy's presence. I guess Tina watches *Hello, today!* and knows who Miranda Monroe is. Emmy must've slipped past me and returned to the store while I was in the closet, searching for Tina's jacket. Tina is captivated by Emmy. Her eyes are wide, and her mouth is ajar, yet smiling.

"You're even prettier in person," Tina gushes with an awestruck expression plastered to her face.

"Thank you," Emmy smiles graciously. "You're gorgeous, by the way. Your complexion is spectacular. Tell me about your skin care regimen."

Being the true professional she is, you'd never guess Emmy is in emotional distress and just spent ten hours travelling. Her superpower is turning off Emmy Garcia and turning on Miranda Monroe with less effort than it takes to flip a light switch.

"Soap and water," Tina giggles with a shrug. "And lots of moisturizer. Especially in the cold months when the air is dry."

"It's all about the moisturizer," my sister agrees.

"Why are you in Harmony Lake?" Tina asks Emmy as I approach them at the counter. "Are you here to buy yarn? Are you a knitter?"

"Our mother taught us both how to knit," Emmy explains, jerking her head toward me. "I go through knitting phases every few years, but I'm not as dedicated as Megan."

"Miranda Monroe is your sister?" Tina asks, staring at me, dumbfounded. "The same sister you worried about this morning?"

"This is her," I confirm, smiling.

"But I thought your sister's name is Emmy?" Tina scrunches her brows together in confusion.

"Emmy is my nickname," my sister explains. "My given name is Miranda, but friends and family call me Emmy. You can call me Emmy." She flashes Tina a thousand-watt smile.

"I can?" Tina asks, mesmerized. "I'm glad you're OK, Emmy. Megan was worried."

Emmy looks at me and puts her hand on mine. "I'm sorry I didn't let you know I was coming ahead of time. It was an impromptu decision." She sighs. "I was incommunicado during the flight. I saw your texts when I landed and meant to reply from the rental car, but I couldn't get my phone to connect to the car, and it's not safe to text and drive. I told myself I'd text you when I pulled over, but I drove straight through. I didn't mean to worry you."

"You're here now," I say.

"Now that I know you're sisters, I can see the resemblance," Tina observes.

Either Tina's skills of observation are superhuman, or the resemblance she claims to see is wishful thinking. There is no resemblance and hasn't been for at least a decade. We used to have the same curly brown hair, but Emmy dyes her hair blonde now. Her colourist does an amazing job. Unless you knew her before her blonde phase, you'd never guess Emmy isn't a natural blonde. And regular Brazilian blowouts keep her curls at bay and ensure her hair is smooth, shiny, and bouncy. Growing up, we had the same fair skin, but regular appointments with a spray tanner give Emmy's complexion a year-round, sun-kissed shimmer. We both inherited our father's hazel eyes, but thanks to the miracle of tinted contact lenses, Emmy's eyes are closer to emerald green than hazel. Our body shapes have always been different. My curvy, hourglass figure is courtesy of our mother, while Emmy inherited her narrow, petite frame and delicate features from our father's side of the family. I've always been jealous of Emmy's ability to wear spaghetti straps without a bra, and I always will be.

The only physical traits Emmy and I still have in common are our height and shoe size. I suspect my sister has had some Botox because her face is suspiciously smooth for forty. She's only sixteen months younger than me, and I'm sure my forehead lines and crow's feet were well-established sixteen months ago. Compared to my sister's mannequin-like skin, my skin looks like it was made by Rand McNally.

"I wish I could stay and hang out with you all afternoon," Tina announces, throwing her jacket over her arm. "But my break is only an hour. If I don't leave now, I'll be late getting back to work."

"I'm sure we'll see each other again," Emmy assures her. "I'll be in town for a few days."

Tina leaves, and with the flip of an invisible switch, television personality Miranda Monroe disappears and my sister, Emmy Garcia takes her place.

"Emmy?" Connie drops her purse on the counter. "What a wonderful surprise." She walks toward Emmy with her arms wide. "We worried when you weren't on *Hello, today!* this morning.

"Hi, Connie." Emmy stands up, and I can tell she's fending off a fresh round of tears.

"Oh, my," Connie says when my sister, sobbing, falls into her arms, leaving an emotional puddle on the hardwood floor. "There, there, Emmy. Shhhh." Connie's blue eyes fill with the moisture of sympathetic tears.

As they sway, Connie smoothes Emmy's hair and murmurs reassuring things.

Connie is in her element. She's the most motherly woman I know, and it's never more obvious than when she unleashes her maternal instincts to comfort someone.

After they pull apart, Emmy explains to Connie that her marriage is over, and she came to Harmony Lake to process everything in a supportive, private environment. Then, worried that another fan might show up and she'll have to flip the magic switch that summons Miranda Monroe, my sister excuses herself again to freshen up.

"Why don't you take Emmy home, my dear," Connie suggests. "She's exhausted. Get her settled in your guest room, and I'll take care of the store."

"Are you sure?" I ask. "I hate to leave you on your own."

"It's not busy today. I'll be fine," Connie insists. "Emmy is distraught. She travelled ten hours for love and support."

"You're right," I admit, feeling guilty for worrying about work when my sister feels like her life is falling apart. "I'll take Emmy home."

CHAPTER 3

I THINK Emmy might be an emotional packer. Is emotional packing a real thing, or did I just make it up? It's like emotional eating except instead of overeating to deal with emotional upheaval, she packs everything in sight for a trip she claims is short.

For someone who says she'll only be in town for a few days, she packed enough stuff to stay forever. Considering her travel history, you'd think she'd have packing down to an efficient science. But Emmy is fragile right now, so I don't tease her about the amount of stuff she brought, or ask her how much she paid the airline for excess baggage fees. Instead, I bite my lip and help lug her collection of suitcases, rolling luggage, and overnight bags from the rental car to the guest room.

"Just a sec," I say when my phone dings in my pocket. I bring the rolling suitcase to its upright position and drop the overnight bag I'm carrying in my other hand on top of it. I slide my phone out of my pocket and look at the screen. "*Hffffftttthhhhhhtttttttttt!*" I suck in my breath through my clenched teeth.

"What?" Emmy asks. "Who is it?"

"Armando."

"The nerve!" She stomps her foot and drops the overnight bag and suitcase she's lugging onto the floor, narrowly missing Sophie, who's prancing around us in excited circles. "Read it to me."

Armando: Hi, Megan. Have you spoken to Emmy? We argued yesterday, and she blocked me. I just need to know she's OK.

"You blocked him?" I ask.

"I don't want to talk to him. Not yet."

"How should I respond?" I ask, dreading placing myself in the middle of their domestic dispute.

Emmy shrugs. "Don't bother." She picks up her suitcase and overnight bag and continues trudging to the guest room.

"I have to tell him something," I plead. "He's worried. And I don't want Armando to keep texting and calling me because he doesn't know where you are. What if he reports you missing or something?"

"Fine." Emmy huffs, once again dropping her suitcase and overnight bag. "But I don't want him to know I'm here."

"You do it." I thrust my phone toward her. "But I want to read it before you send it, since he thinks it's from me."

Emmy takes the phone, and after several minutes of typing, reading aloud, discussing, backspacing, and retyping she replies with:

Me: Emmy is fine. She is taking some time for herself. She'll be in touch when she's ready.

Another moment of brief deliberation, and Emmy hits send.

"There," she says, foisting the phone at me. "Done." She lets out a long, wistful sigh.

I slip the phone into my pocket, and we finish hauling her physical baggage to the guest room.

We stash the luggage out of the way because Emmy is too exhausted—physically and mentally—to deal with it now. She says she'll unpack and organize her belongings after she has a bath, something to eat, and a nap.

While Emmy soaks in a hot bath with Himalayan bath salts, Sophie and I go for a walk around the block, then I make lunch. Tomato soup and grilled cheese sandwiches, comfort food from our childhood. Our mother used to make it for us on cold winter days.

During lunch, Emmy yawns and rubs her eyes, picking at her soup and sandwich until she excuses herself for a nap.

"Eric is golfing so the house will be quiet, and no one will bother you," I tell her. "I might go back to the store. If you need me, call or text."

Emmy gives me a tight hug and tells me not to worry.

"Can Sophie stay with me?"

"That's up to Sophie," I reply.

My sister gets a glass of water, then heads to the guest room with Sophie following behind her. I'm not surprised; Sophie loves naps. The padding of feet and paws gets fainter until they disappear, and the bedroom door closes with a dull thud.

KNITORIOUS ISN'T BUSY, and Connie makes an entire Knitted Knocker while I empty the bulky yarn shelves, wash them, then re-shelve the bulky yarn.

"I hope she's still there when we get back," April says into my Airpods, disappointed about missing my sister.

"I doubt she'll stay a full week," I say. "She loves her job, and she'll miss it. But if she stays, she brought more than enough stuff with her." I explain how a reality show is the crux of my sister's disagreement with her husband, and I'm optimistic that they'll work it out. "A bit of time, rest, and a little distance will give them some perspective," I suggest.

"*Perfect Match* is our favourite show," April confesses. "We record it on the PVR so we won't miss an episode."

"Really?" I'm stunned. "You've never mentioned it before."

"It's a guilty pleasure," April says. "Watching other people's lives fall apart and judging their decisions makes me feel better about my boring, routine existence."

"Your life is neither boring nor routine."

"I know," April replies, "but compared to the couples on *Perfect Match*, it is."

"Do you vote?"

"Every week," April declares with pride. "We have the app on our phones. We vote at the end of each episode. But we're never right. The couple we vote for is never the couple that the host evicts. It's weird. Even in the online forums, masses of viewers will agree which couple should get the boot, but it's hardly ever the couple they evict. I guess the people who vote for the right couple don't post about it on social media."

"Weird," I agree, arranging yarn skeins on the newly cleaned shelf.

April tells me about her cousin's wedding dress, and the cake they made for the big day, and I'm vaguely aware of the jingle over the door behind me. When I glance at Connie, she looks at me wide-eyed. She gives her head an almost indiscernible jerk toward the counter, and by instinct, I look in that direction.

"Armando?" I ask, incredulous. I hold up my index finger, signaling to Armando that I'll be right with him. "April, I have to go. I'll call you back."

"Is that Armando?" April asks, keen for details.

"Uh-huh." I nod, even though she can't see me. "I'll call you back."

"You better! I want to know everything," April insists. "They'd be great on *Perfect Match*. They could win. Just saying."

"Bye," I say.

"Bye, Megastar."

April likes to come up with nicknames that are puns of my actual name. Today, I'm Megastar.

"Hi, Megan," Armando says.

"How did you get here so fast? We just texted an hour ago."

"I was on my way to Harmony Lake when I texted you. I was hoping Emmy might unblock me, but she didn't. Not yet."

Armando is two years younger than my sister, but he looks younger than his thirty-eight years. His skin is flawless, and he's in optimal physical shape, thanks to the trainers, coaches, and dieticians who keep him on a strict fitness and food regimen. His dark hair is styled in one of those trendy, too-much-on-top hairstyles where the top somewhat resembles a bird's nest and is longer than the sides and back. Also, Armando wears trendy active wear and footwear, provided free by sponsors who want him to be seen and photographed wearing their gear.

"Well… it's nice to see you." I smile and shrug.

"Same here." Armando advances toward me with his arms open.

I wipe my hands on my thighs and remove my Airpods. Armando and I greet each other with a double-cheek kiss and a hug.

"You remember, Connie," I say, gesturing to the chair where Connie is casting on another brown Knitted Knocker.

"Of course, I remember Connie." Grinning, Armando opens his arms. "I never forget a beautiful woman," he says, closing in on her.

She leaves her knitting on the chair and greets Armando with the standard hug and double-cheek kiss.

"Aren't you a silver-tongued devil?"

I detect a hint of sarcasm in her voice.

Connie offers to get us refreshments, and I invite Armando to take a seat in the cozy sitting area.

"Why are you here?"

"To see my wife."

"What makes you think she's here?"

"I used the find my friends app on our phones," Armando explains. "It's the only thing Emmy didn't block me from." A rolled r sneaks into the last word of his sentence.

Armando is from Ecuador, but he's lived away from Ecuador longer than he lived there. Years ago, he had elocution lessons to minimize his accent. This was at the suggestion of his agent who told him it would help him get sponsorship deals.

"If you used the find my friends app, you know Emmy isn't at Knitorious," I point out, realizing that when he texted me earlier, worried about his missing wife, he knew darn well she was at my house and that I had spoken to her. "Why didn't you go to her location? Why are you here?"

"Emmy made it clear she's not ready to see me yet," Armando says. "I don't want to upset her more. Also, I'm tired from the journey. It's best for both of us to get some rest before we talk. But I wanted to ask how she is and tell you I'm here."

I hope he doesn't expect me to breach my sister's confidence or side with him. Whether or not I agree with Emmy, she's my sister and my loyalty lies with her.

"I see," I acknowledge, staying neutral.

It's brighter than usual in the store because the windows are spotless—if I say so myself. Glancing toward the window, I'm struck by how exposed we are. There's not much blocking the view of the cozy sitting area from the sidewalk or the street,and Emmy and Armando take constant precautions to protect their privacy.

"Let's go in the back," I suggest, standing up.

Armando follows me to the back room, and we run into Connie. She's carrying a tray of tea and biscuits. Taking the tray from her, I thank her for the refreshments and tell her we'll sit in the kitchenette because there's more privacy and no windows. Smiling, she leaves us alone, closing the door that separates the store from the backroom.

Armando and I make small talk about the tea, the biscuits, then the weather. Our small talk is slow and awkward. We take turns searching for topics, with each of us struggling to keep up our respective ends of the conversation. It's obvious Armando and I don't really know each other. In fact, I think this is the first time we've been alone together. Until today, we've only seen each other at group gatherings. Aside from pleasantries about weather, Hannah, or soccer, we've never had a one-on-one conversation longer than a couple of minutes.

"Did Emmy tell you what we disagreed about?" Armando asks, addressing the elephant in the room.

"Yes."

"I would say yes if I could," Armando says, shrugging one shoulder. I assume he's referring to the *Perfect*

27

Match opportunity. "But I have a contract. I'm obligated to my team." He dips a biscuit in his tea, bobbing it up and down. "As far as professional soccer players go, I'm old. Over the hill. I'm one of the oldest in the league. This could be my last season. I want to go out on top. I can't afford to miss training camp or the preseason. I have to work harder than ever to stay on top of my game and keep up with the younger players."

"Did you tell this to Emmy?" I ask.

"I tried," Armando says with a sigh. "She didn't want to hear it."

"I see." I repeat my neutral, don't get involved response.

"I'm not sure how to resolve this with her."

"I don't know what to tell you," I say, shaking my head and placing my empty cup and plate on the tray. "It's not my place to get involved."

"Of course," Armando agrees. "I would never put you in the middle." Following my lead, he places his dishes on the tea tray. "But I know how much Emmy respects your opinion. She listens to you… "

I raise my hand in a stop motion, cutting him off midsentence.

"My sister knows her own mind and makes her own decisions. I would never manipulate her."

"You misunderstand. I would never ask you to." He smiles, flashing his shiny, straight, super-white teeth. Armando looks at his watch and stands up. "I should go. It's getting late."

"I'll tell Emmy you were here." I say, accompanying him to the back door.

28

"I expect nothing less," Armando says. "Please tell her I'm staying at the Rise & Glide Resort and Spa. I'd text her with my room number, but she blocked me."

The Rise & Glide is a ski resort in the Harmony Hills mountains. It's only twenty minutes away by car, and it's the most upscale accommodation within driving distance.

"Great choice. Rise & Glide was recently renovated. I hear the rooms are beautiful."

"I've never stayed there," Armando says. "Brad booked the suite for me. He says the online reviews and photos were good, and I trust his judgement. Also, it has a state-of-the-art fitness facility, so I can keep up with my training while I'm here."

I interpret this to mean that Armando has confided in Brad about his and Emmy's marital issues. How else would Armando explain why he needed somewhere to stay at the last minute in Harmony Lake?

After another hug and another double-cheek kiss, Armando leaves through the back door.

"WHERE'S ARMANDO?" Connie asks when I return to the store after cleaning up the tea and biscuit dishes.

"He went out the back."

"What did he want from you?" She crosses her arms in front of her chest and quirks an eyebrow.

"What makes you think he wanted something?"

I mean, she's not wrong, but how did Connie know Armando had an agenda?

"I've met his type before," she cautions with an air of wisdom. "They use flattery, persuasion, and charm to pull the wool over your eyes."

"Armando *is* quite charming and flattering," I agree.

"After three years of being your brother-in-law, why would he suddenly show up acting like he visits all the time?"

"I suspect he wanted me to persuade Emmy to see his side of their disagreement," I admit. "I said no and told him I won't get involved."

"Good girl." Connie lifts her chin and flashes me a proud smirk.

"Now, which shelves should I clean next?" I mutter, tapping my chin and searching my imagination for inspiration. "It's missing something, isn't it?"

"We'll decide tomorrow, my dear," Connie responds to my rhetorical question as she locks the door and turns the sign from OPEN to CLOSED.

CHAPTER 4

SATURDAY, October 2nd

It's still dark outside when I wake up surrounded by silence. I pull the covers up to my chin and hunker down, cocooning myself in the goose-down duvet and flannel sheets. Comfy, I bask in the warm silence and try to will myself back to sleep. Nope. I'm wide awake. When I close my eyes, items from my to-do list flash in my mind's eye. *Sigh.* I reach one arm outside my cocoon and stretch it across the bed, searching for Sophie. Nothing but the duvet.

"Sophie?" I ask, lifting my head off the pillow and searching the dark bed for her corgi-shaped silhouette. "Soph?" Nothing.

I wrap my pink fluffy robe around me, slip into my white fluffy slippers, and shuffle toward the coffeemaker. Someone has already made coffee. Wafts of caffeine-infused air guide my nose when I turn the corner toward the kitchen.

"Morning, Sis!" Emmy smiles from the corner of the

family room sofa. She's curled up with her feet under her butt. The afghan from the back of the sofa covers her legs, and she's leafing through a magazine. Sophie nestles into Emmy's hip, resting her head on Emmy's thigh.

"Good morning," I say. "You're up early."

"Um, excuse me?" She snorts with a chuckle. "I've been up for a while. After years of getting up for work in the middle of the night, my body doesn't remember how to sleep in."

Sophie jumps down from the sofa and trots toward me, tail wagging, to say good morning.

"I always forget," I admit, bending down to rub Sophie. "I still associate you with the teenager who refused to drag her butt out of bed before noon."

"Those days are long gone," Emmy quips, turning the page. "Sophie's been out already, but I haven't fed her."

"Thanks," I say, rummaging through the basket of coffee pods until I find one that will hit the spot: French Vanilla.

I hold up the pod and look at Emmy, wordlessly offering her a coffee. In response, she holds up her mug and smiles, indicating that she already has a coffee.

While the coffeemaker transforms the coffee pod into liquid heaven, I fix Sophie's breakfast and put it on the floor. She digs in and doesn't come up for air until her bowl is empty.

"Your fiancé went for an early morning run," Emmy advises when I join her on the sofa.

"He's weird like that," I respond, tugging the afghan until I have enough to cover the bottom of my legs.

"How's the wedding planning coming along?" my sister asks.

I shrug, swallowing a mouthful of coffee. "It isn't," I admit. "We haven't discussed it, or picked a date, or anything."

"I assumed from this pile of wedding magazines that you were in wedding-planning mode." Emmy gestures to the tall pile of glossy magazines on the coffee table.

"I didn't buy those," I confess. "People give them to me. Each magazine is a not-so-subtle hint that we have to get a wiggle on and plan our wedding."

"It sounds like you aren't in a hurry," Emmy says, closing the bridal magazine she was leafing through and tossing on top of the pile.

"I'm not," I admit. "But Eric would like to move things along." I sigh. "There's so much to plan. Even a small wedding is a lot of work."

"You could always elope like Armando and I," she suggests, grinning. "I can give you the contact information for the adorable chapel we went to in Vegas. Just choose what to wear and show up. They take care of flowers, photography, everything. They even have a package that includes wedding rings."

"It sounds tempting." I take another sip of coffee. "Is that why you eloped? Because you didn't want to plan a wedding?"

"I would've loved to plan our wedding," Emmy professes. "Eloping was Armando's idea." She breaks

33

into a sheepish grin. "He's very romantic, you know. He wanted our wedding to be private and intimate. He said he didn't want to share me with anyone else, and he wanted us to focus on each other instead of details." She blushes as she recalls her wedding.

"I didn't realize he was so sentimental."

"He didn't even want to tell anyone we got married," she adds.

"You never told me this. Why didn't he want anyone to know?"

"He said he wanted it to be our secret. Something special that only we shared. He's a very private person, Sis. Private and romantic."

"But your marriage is public knowledge, so I assume he came around to your way of thinking?"

"We agreed to tell people, and we had a reception when we got home from our honeymoon. I think Armando would've been happier to keep it between us, but he wanted me to be happy, so we compromised." She blushes and grins again, this time looking wistfully at her wedding ring.

I remember the reception well. It was a beautiful formal event in the ballroom of a fancy hotel.

"Do you regret eloping?" I ask as Sophie leaps onto the sofa, licking her chops, and turning in circles before she lies down.

"No." Emmy shrugs. "We had the reception afterward, and a big wedding would have been awkward with his family and stuff."

"Because they're in Ecuador?"

"That and because he doesn't talk to them."

"He doesn't?" This is the first I've heard of relationship issues between Armando and his family. "Why not?"

Emmy shrugs. "It happened before Armando and I met. I don't know all the details, and Armando doesn't like to talk about it, but he said they disagreed over money. Armando's money. He said they weren't happy with how much he gave them. He got tired of fighting, cut them off financially, and they retaliated by cutting off all communication with him."

"That's awful," I sympathize. "Poor Armando."

"I know." My sister nods. "I'm literally his only family. And since his family turned his best friend against him, he doesn't have any friends from his old life either."

"His family turned his best friend against him?"

"Armando said his family tried to get his best friend to side with them about the money issue, and it destroyed their friendship. He said it was bound to happen sooner or later because their relationship became strained because his friend was jealous when Armando made the major leagues. His friend didn't get a chance to play for the majors because he had a career-ending knee injury."

"Poor guy."

My sister nods. "I think that's why Brad's friendship is so important to him. He doesn't want to lose anyone else."

"Your attitude toward Armando this morning is warmer than yesterday," I observe, wondering if reminiscing about their elopement is the reason. "Does this mean you might unblock him?"

"I already unblocked him," Emmy admits with a smirk. "Last night after you told me he visited you at Knitorious."

"You blocked his calls, you blocked him on social media, and you blocked his texts, but you didn't block him from your Find My Friends app. That was on purpose, wasn't it?"

I've been wanting to ask her this since yesterday. My sister is too strategic and too smart for such an oversight.

"Guilty." She holds her hands up in a conciliatory gesture. "I wanted to see if he'd follow me to Harmony Lake."

"Like a test?" I ask.

"Sort of," Emmy admits. Then she swats my arm. "Don't judge me."

"I'm not judging, I swear."

April might be right when she said Emmy and Armando could win *Perfect Match*.

"I spoke to him last night before bed. We're meeting today to talk."

"He's welcome to come here," I offer.

"Thanks, Sis, but I'm meeting him for breakfast in his hotel suite. The fewer people who know we're in town, the better. We don't need any speculation about our relationship while we work this out."

"Call me if you need anything," I remind her. "And you're welcome to stay here as long as you want."

THE STORE IS SO busy my brain has stopped registering the jingle of the bell over the door. It opens and closes so often, that if I looked up every time I heard it, I'd never look at anything else.

"Are you having a sale or something?" Eric asks when he and Sophie enter the store. "It's busier than usual." He hands me a chocolate caramel latte.

"Thank you for the coffee." I give him a quick kiss. "We're not having a sale," I answer his question. "It's been busy since we opened. It doesn't help that Connie and I are rushed off our feet because Marla is working at the bakery."

"And she says the bakery is just as busy as Knitorious," Connie interjects, breezing past us with a customer in tow. "Apparently all the businesses on Water Street are busier than usual today. No one knows why," Connie adds, piling skeins of peppermint pink baby yarn into her customer's arms. "It's a mystery." She shrugs.

"What are you and Sophie up to?" I ask, sorting some skeins of mislaid sock yarn.

"It was time for Sophie's walk, and she wanted to surprise you with a coffee," he explains, looking around the store at the bustle of browsing knitters.

"She's such a thoughtful dog," I say, looking at Sophie. She wags her butt, panting at me.

"I told Emmy I'd help her move her stuff to Armando's suite at Rise & Glide, but I can come back after and help," he offers. "I can work the cash register, or put stuff away, or whatever."

"That's sweet," I say. "Thank you."

"Have you spoken to Emmy?" Eric asks, following me from the shelves of sock yarn to the racks of knitting needles, so I can re-shelve some knitting needles that a customer abandoned in the sock-yarn section.

"She phoned a little while ago," I reply. "I couldn't talk because the store was too busy, but she said Armando agreed to talk to the network and his team management about *Perfect Match*. And he agreed to fire Brad and look for another agent. An agent Emmy and Armando both like. I'm glad they found a compromise."

A knitter with a sweater pattern from 1987 interrupts Eric's account of how Emmy's luggage seems to have multiplied since she arrived yesterday.

"I'm afraid this yarn company went out of business twenty-five years ago," I explain when the knitter asks if we carry the yarn used in the pattern. I direct her to the worsted weight section and tell her I'll be right over to help her find a suitable substitution. "I'm sorry, I have to get back to work," I tell Eric. "Thank you for helping Emmy. Mind your back when you lift the luggage, it's heavier than it looks." I give Sophie a quick scratch between the ears, and they leave.

CHAPTER 5

SUNDAY, October 3rd

This is my first visit to The Rise & Glide Resort since their renovations. It was renovated inside and out. The old Rise & Glide had a rustic aesthetic, reminiscent of a hunting lodge. The new, rebranded Rise & Glide Resort and Retreat is sleek and modern.

"Nice," I whisper as I enter the main lobby, greeted by calming neutral colours, clean lines, and sophisticated yet comfortable furnishings.

I could've stayed in the car and sent Emmy a text to let her know I'm here, but curiosity got the better of me.

"Megan? Is that you?"

I turn my head left, then right, searching for the source of my name.

"Deb?" I confirm when I recognize the face that matches the voice. "What are you doing here?"

"I'm the resort manager," Deb explains. "Haven't you heard? I oversaw the entire renovation." She gestures proudly around her.

"Wow." Deb and I hug. "You did an amazing job. It's beautiful."

"Thank you," Deb replies, her blushing cheeks a sharp contrast to her blonde hair with silver highlights.

Deb Kee is a modest lady, who's uncomfortable receiving compliments, even when they're well deserved. A lifetime resident of Harmony Lake, Deb recently retired from the Harmony Lake Fire Department. She is one of the many strong, pioneering women who call Harmony Lake home. Besides working in a traditionally male occupation, she was the HLFD's first ever female Firefighter of the Year. Deb Kee blazed a trail—pun intended—for the generations of female firefighters who came after her.

"I thought you retired," I say. "Connie said you were living it up in a retirement community with your rescue dogs."

Deb lets out a short, shrill whistle, and two dogs, a Miniature Pinscher and a Collie mix, trot out from behind the registration counter and stand by their owner's side.

"Retirement is overrated," Deb says while I crouch down to rub Blitz and Abby. "Besides, this isn't work, it's fun."

"I hope I have your zest for life when it's my time to retire," I comment.

"Are you here to see the ballroom?" Deb asks after some small talk and local gossip.

I shake my head. "I wasn't planning on it."

Deb asks with such confidence that I second guess

myself and wonder if I *am* supposed to see the ballroom.

"Connie said if you come by I should show you the ballroom," Deb explains. "She said if you say no, I should show you, anyway."

"Ahh." I nod. "Connie did mention it would make an ideal wedding venue."

Connie mentions the wedding a lot; I swear she thinks about it more than me.

"It would be a beautiful wedding venue, Megan. And we offer a range of wedding packages. Our event planner doesn't work Sundays, but I'd be happy to give you a quick tour, and we could look at dates if you know what time of year… "

"Thanks, Deb," I interrupt her Connie-motivated sales pitch. "But I'm here to pick up my sister. She and her husband are guests. We have a brunch date. I'd love to look at the ballroom, but Adam's expecting us. I promise to come back with Eric for a tour."

"Are you sure?" Deb asks, undeterred. "Connie said…"

"Don't worry," I assure her. "I'll tell Connie you tried. And Eric and I will meet with the event planner… soon." I smile.

Deb, Blitz, and Abby walk me to the elevator. While I wait for the door to open, Deb points out some features and special touches she insisted on during the renovation. She has my undivided attention when she tells me about the renovated spa on the sixth floor.

Deb's cell phone buzzes, and she looks at the screen. Worry lines corrugate her forehead.

"Enjoy your brunch, Megan. I have to go."

"Is everything OK?" I ask.

"Another staff member came down with that bug that's going around. She has to go home sick, and we're already understaffed."

"What kind of bug?" I wonder out loud, silently hoping there's a bottle of hand sanitizer in my purse.

"A gastrointestinal thing. The housekeeping staff call it gut rot." Deb flicks her wrist like something called gut rot is nothing more than a minor inconvenience. "At least it's happening now instead of in the middle of ski season." She shrugs.

Deb's always optimistic. Who else could find a silver lining in a gut-rot outbreak among her employees?

"Take care, Deb. I hope you don't get it."

"Don't worry about me, Megan. I have a cast-iron gut." She chuckles and rubs her belly.

"SHHH," Emmy greets me by bringing her index finger to her lips and shushing me.

I nod and pretend to zip my lips with my thumb and forefinger.

"Armando is asleep," she explains in a whisper. "He's dead to the world." She beckons me inside, then closes the door without making a sound. "Wait here," she mouths holding her index finger in the air. "I'll be right back."

I reply with a wink and a thumbs up. Emmy disappears into what I assume is the bedroom and reappears a moment later with her purse slung over her shoulder.

We exit the suite, making as little noise as possible and head toward the elevator.

"Armando needs his sleep," Emmy says in her normal tone of voice, hooking her arm through mine and pulling me close so she can speak into my ear. "We were up late last night making up," she gushes, nudging my ribs and winking. "He's exhausted!" She giggles.

"Ew," I blurt, laughing and covering my ears with my hands. "Too much information! There are some things I don't need to know."

We laugh and speed up our pace when the elevator door opens. Still giggling, we pass an employee pushing a cart with a covered tray.

"Good morning, ladies," he says with a nod when he passes us.

"Good morning," we reply in unison.

"WHATEVER IT IS, IT SMELLS AMAZING!" Emmy declares when I ask Adam what we're having for brunch.

"It's a surprise," Adam teases from the kitchen of his condo.

Adam and I have brunch every Sunday. We alternate between his condo and my house, but Adam always cooks. Our daughter, Hannah, joins us on video chat from her dorm room in Toronto. It was awkward at first, but Adam and I worked hard to come through our separation and divorce as friends. Our marriage is over, but we're still co-parents, and we'll always be family. We still love each other, but not the way spouses should. Our marriage didn't end with a dramatic bang, it fizzled slowly, over many years. We either didn't notice, or ignored the signs until it was too late. Attempts to reignite the spark were futile, and we admitted we would be happier unmarried. Our divorce isn't traditional, but it works for us, and it works for our daughter, which is all that matters.

"If you won't tell us what it is, how should I set the table?" I ask, trying to peek around him as he blocks the stove with his body. Unsuccessful, I stand on my tippy toes and try to look over his shoulder. Also unsuccessful. Instead of brunch, I get a close-up view of his salt and pepper hair.

"Set it with the standard stuff," he suggests.

"Plates or bowls?" Emmy asks. "Forks or spoons? Will we need knives? Regular knives or steak knives?" She pelts him with rapid-fire questions.

"Fine," Adam declares, defeated. "We're having Green Toad-In-The-Hole.

We scrunch up our faces in a way that lets Adam know the name isn't as appetizing as the aroma.

"I made it up," he explains with a one-shoulder shrug. "I didn't know what to call it and thought Green Toad-In-The-Hole sounded trendy." Emmy and I shake our heads. Frustrated, Adam huffs and furrows his thick brows. "I made a spinach-artichoke-cream cheese spread," he explains, and I resist my urge to dip my finger in the yummy-looking spread when he shows it to us. "Then I cut a hole in the centre of thick-slices of crusty bread and spread the cream-cheese mixture on the bread. I cracked an egg in the hole, sprinkled with grated Gruyère cheese, and baked it in the oven."

"Wow! It looks incredible, Adam," I assure him. "But it needs a better name."

His blue eyes gleam with pride at the compliment.

"Can you send me the recipe?" Emmy asks. "Armando would love this."

My ex-husband's culinary skills have come a long way since we separated. When we lived together, Adam couldn't cook anything beyond heating leftovers in the microwave—with specific instructions. And now, he's inventing restaurant-worthy recipes.

While I set the table, Emmy uses Adam's tablet to contact Hannah on video chat. Hannah doesn't know her Aunt Emmy is joining us for brunch today. Emmy's visit is as much a surprise to my daughter today as it was to me at Knitorious on Friday.

Hannah and Aunt Emmy are thrilled to see each other. They spend most of the meal talking to each other while Adam and I enjoy our Green Toad-In-The-Hole free from conversation. Though, we're able to squeeze in a short visit with our daughter before she announces she has to go and ends the video call.

"I know a great entertainment lawyer. I'll send you her contact information," Adam offers when, over a second cup of coffee, Emmy tells him about their opportunity to appear on *Perfect Match*.

"You're the only lawyer I trust, Adam," Emmy

responds. "You've handled every legal need I've ever had. I'd rather deal with you."

It's true. Adam has represented Emmy in two divorces and three real estate transactions. He drew up her will and powers of attorney, and helped negotiate her contract with *Hello, today*!

"Don't sign anything until I've looked at it," Adam counsels in his lawyer-voice.

"I know, Adam."

Emmy's tone of voice and eye-roll reminds me of our petulant teenage years when we used the same tone of voice and eye-roll with our parents.

"Promise?" Adam asks, now using his dad-voice.

"I won't sign anything until you say so." She flashes a sarcastic grin, then her phone chimes. "It's Poppy," Emmy announces, standing up. "I have to take this." She looks at Adam. "Can I step onto the balcony?"

"Of course," Adam replies. "The door's unlocked."

Poppy Prescott is Emmy's best friend and personal assistant. They've known each other since university. Emmy and Poppy complement each other's strengths and weaknesses. Poppy is an introvert who encourages Emmy to slow down and engage in occasional introspection. Emmy is an extrovert who encourages Poppy to step outside her comfort zone and interact with people more than she would without Emmy pressuring her. Poppy is a planner. She takes her time making decisions and weighs the pros and cons of her options. Emmy is impulsive and prone to acting or speaking before she thinks.

The door to the balcony closes with Emmy on the other side, and Adam leans into me.

"I'm worried, Meg."

"About Emmy?"

He nods. "She's too excited about this *Perfect Match* thing. I'm afraid she'll agree to whatever they offer, and it won't be in her best interest."

"I had the same thought," I admit.

"You know how spontaneous she is."

"Yes, I do," I agree, recalling how she spontaneously arrived on my doorstep two days ago.

"Do you think it's possible she already signed something?" Adam asks. "It would explain why she's so desperate to get Armando to agree."

"She's impulsive, Adam, but I don't think she'd sign anything without at least talking to her husband and lawyer first," I argue. "You've intervened on her behalf more than once to undo her bad decisions. I'm sure she learned from those mistakes."

Plural. More than one mistake. My sister has a habit of committing, then regretting.

"I don't know, Meg," Adam says, with an undertone of concern. "She married her first two husbands just weeks after she met them. She eloped with Armando a few months after they met and before I could draw up a prenuptial agreement. She almost signed a horrible contract with *Hello, today!*..."

"OK, Adam. I get it," I say, interrupting his verbal inventory of my sister's questionable decisions.

"She needs a babysitter." Adam arches his thick eyebrows and leans back in his chair.

"That's what Poppy does," I remind him. "She's the stabilizing voice of reason in Emmy's hectic life."

Poppy is an unsung hero. She's talked my sister off more than one proverbial ledge. I don't know what Emmy would do without her.

"I wish Mum and Dad handled their divorce more like you guys and less like World War III," Emmy comments out of nowhere when she returns from the balcony.

"Me too," I admit. "But divorce is traumatic regardless of how friendly it is. I just hope Hannah is less traumatized than we were."

"She is," Emmy reassures me. "Hannah's resilient like us." She smiles.

"Hannah will never know the pain and toxicity of parents who hate each other and can't interact with each other," Adam adds, giving my hand a quick squeeze.

Though he's not a child of divorce, Adam specialized in family law for many years and saw firsthand how divorce can bring out the worst in people. The emotions that accompany a nasty divorce can have a ripple effect throughout a family, destroying generations of relationships. Over the years, I've often heard him remind clients that *the person you marry and the person you divorce are not the same person*. It's one of the truest things I've ever heard.

"Here's hoping our family doesn't experience any more divorces," I say, hoping to shut down the topic on an optimistic note.

I stand up and start piling dishes to clear the table.

"I won't get divorced again," Emmy declares with confidence as she stands up and helps me clear the table. "I refuse. I'd rather be widowed than go through another divorce."

CHAPTER 6

"How long are you staying in town?" I ask Emmy on the drive back to Rise & Glide.

"That's what I talked to Poppy about," Emmy replies. "Hannah mentioned that she's coming home for Thanksgiving next weekend. I'd like to stay and have Thanksgiving with the family. I'm not sure if Armando can stay, but Poppy is talking to the producers *at Hello, today!* to arrange for someone to cover for me next week."

In Canada, we celebrate Thanksgiving a month earlier than our American friends.

"Really?" I ask, surprised. "I can't remember the last time we had Thanksgiving together! Yay!"

"I hope Armando can stay," Emmy adds. "It would be nice for him to spend quality time with everyone. You should get to know each other better."

"I hope he can stay too," I agree. "You could stay way past Thanksgiving. You packed enough stuff to stay for at least a year," I tease.

"I wasn't thinking straight," Emmy explains, laughing. "I just grabbed whatever I saw and threw it in a bag until I ran out of bags." She bursts into a fresh fit of giggles. "Eric's eyes almost popped out of his head when he saw all my luggage. I'm sure he regretted offering to help me carry it."

"Here we are," I say, pulling into the parking lot.

"Can you come upstairs for a minute? I got swag bags for you and Hannah at that awards show I presented at last month. If I don't give them to you now, I'll forget."

"I always have time to collect swag bags," I reply, unbuckling my seatbelt.

A swag bag is a gift bag given to event attendees. My sister says they're common at awards shows. Companies fill the bags with promotional products, hoping the influential people who receive them will use the products and maybe post about them on social media, or get photographed using them. Sometimes, attendees get more than one bag, and when that happens, Emmy grabs extra for Poppy, me, or Hannah.

I leave my purse in the car and just bring my cell phone with me. As we walk from the car to the hotel, my sister pulls out her phone and starts typing.

"Just giving Armando a heads-up that we're on our way upstairs. In case he's not decent." She twitches her eyebrows at me.

At the elevator, she unlocks her phone again.

"Hmph," she says. "Armando always texts me back." She turns the screen toward me. "The message is unread. He hasn't even seen it."

"Maybe he's still sleeping," I suggest with a shrug.

"Uh-uh," Emmy says as we leave the elevator. "Armando lives a very regimented life. He eats the same food at the same time every day and adheres to a strict training routine. There's no way he's still in bed."

"Gym?" I suggest.

"Maybe," Emmy says, checking the time on her phone.

She removes the DO NOT DISTURB sign from the door handle and uses her keycard to unlock the door. I follow her into the room.

Where did the DO NOT DISTURB sign come from? I don't remember seeing it when I was here earlier, and I don't remember Emmy hanging it up when we left. Was it there, and I didn't notice it? Did Armando hang it up after we left?

"The bedroom door is still closed." I point to the closed door. "Maybe he *is* asleep. Maybe you tired him out more than you thought," I tease.

"I'll be right back," she says, ignoring my joke.

Emmy disappears behind the closed door, and I look around the renovated luxury hotel suite. The blackout curtains are closed, and the room is dark. I find a switch on the wall in the sitting area and flip it. A floor lamp next to the sofa lights up, casting a soft glow on the fixtures and furnishings. Everything looks high end. There are more plants than you'd expect in a hotel suite. Are they real or fake? It's hard to tell. I focus on a Boston fern sitting on a round end table near the balcony door. The fern could be an authentic-looking fake, or a real fern so perfect it looks fake. I rub a frond between my thumb and forefinger. It feels real, but I'm not one hundred percent convinced. I pat the soil with my finger then rub my damp finger with my thumb. The fern is real.

Tucked in behind the bushy plant, I notice the corner of a small box. I lift a few fronds out of the way for a closer look. It's an empty cigarette package. Weird. Emmy doesn't smoke, and I assume Armando doesn't smoke. Professional athletes don't smoke, do they? He didn't smell of cigarette smoke when he was at Knitorious on Friday. He hugged Connie, and if she'd picked up a whiff of cigarette smoke, she would have mentioned it after he left. I'm a non-smoker, and I'm sensitive to the specific scent of cigarette smoke. I notice it right away, often from a distance. Especially at work because I don't want it near the yarn. Second-hand smoke—and even third-hand smoke—clings. It clings to clothes, hair, pets, and yarn. No one wants to buy nicotine-infused yarn.

Maybe a previous guest left this cigarette package behind and housekeeping missed it. It would be easy to overlook; I wouldn't have noticed it if I wasn't futzing with the fern.

"Megan." My sister appears behind me like she came out of nowhere.

"What's wrong?" Her eyes are wide and blank. "Emmy?" I touch her hand. It's freezing. "Emmy, what happened?"

"Armando," her limp, cold hand points behind her. "He's not asleep, but he's not awake. He won't answer me."

Oh no! A bowling-ball-sized knot forms in my belly, and impending doom radiates throughout my body.

"No, no, no, no," I mutter under my breath as I step around my sister and lock my gaze on the ajar bedroom door.

"Armando?" I call out. "If this is a joke, it's not funny." The room is dark. I grope the wall just inside the door, find a switch, and flip it. It turns on a dim lamp on the desk in the corner of the room. Great, a lamp that creates ambience instead of actual light. I'm sure it's one of those lamps with multiple levels of brightness, but I'm not interested in figuring out how to adjust it right now. "Armando?" I call out louder than last time.

As my eyes adjust to the darkness, I'm able to make out Armando's silhouette. He's in bed, lying on his back, covered up to his mid-chest. His arms are at his sides outside the covers, and he's facing the window. He's not moving. I walk around the foot of the bed, bump into the room service cart, push it out of my way, and reach for the blackout curtains, tearing them open and squinting at the harsh, sudden invasion of daylight.

"Armando!" I shout.

His eyes are open and glassy. His jaw is slack, and cream-coloured foam coats the corners of his parted lips. He's too still.

"What's wrong with him?" Emmy charges into the room. She races around the foot of the bed, almost tripping over the room service cart, and leans over her husband. "Armando!" She taps the side of his face. No response. "He's not dead," Emmy declares, glaring at me like she's challenging me to defy her.

I pick up the receiver of the landline next to the bed and wait for the dial tone. No dial tone. Do I press 9? How do hotel phones work again? Instead of a dial tone, a man's voice comes on the line.

"Good day, Mr. Garcia. You've reached the front desk. How can I help you?"

"Er. *Ahem*." The lump in my throat blocks my words from coming out, and I clear my throat. "This isn't Mr. Garcia," I manage as I stretch over the bed and place my index and middle fingers on Armando's cool neck.

"Mrs. Garcia?"

"No," I reply, moving my fingers and hoping to feel the pulsating throb of life through Armando's body. "Mr. Garcia needs medical help."

"Ambulance?"

"Yes" I reply, still feeling around for a pulse but not finding one. "And the coroner."

CHAPTER 7

DEB KEE BURSTS into the room carrying a first aid kit and portable AED.

An AED, or automated external defibrillator, is a medical device that delivers a jolt of electricity through two paddles into the patient's chest to jump start the heart.

"Mr. Garcia?" Deb shouts as she rushes past Emmy and I to get to him. "Armando! Can you hear me?"

"Deb is a trained first responder," I whisper to Emmy, pulling her away from Armando so Deb can do her thing. "She knows what she's doing."

My sister and I squeeze together at the bottom of the bed. Deb isn't opening her first aid kit or rushing to use the defibrillator on Armando. She's searching his neck for a pulse, just like I did moments before. She moves her search to his exposed wrist. This isn't good.

A wave of nausea ripples from my stomach to my throat, and I'm suddenly hyper-aware of my senses. My heart pounding in my ears is the loudest thing in the room. The sunlight's glaring intensity forces me to squint. My sister's shaky hand is ice cold, and every time I inhale the smell of the food on the room-service tray next to me, it makes my stomach churn.

Sadly, I have more crime scene experience than a yarn store owner should, and I'm aware it's a no-no to touch anything unless absolutely necessary. But, thanks to the sudden and intense exaggeration of my senses, the slightest hint of the leftover food causes the Green Toad-In-The-Hole to threaten an imminent reappearance. Holding my breath, I reach for the dome-shaped cloche on the bottom shelf of the cart and use it to cover the plate of half-eaten food, then swallow hard, hoping it's enough to push the nausea down.

"Nooooooo!" Emmy shrieks and covers her mouth with her hand when Deb looks up at us, frowning and shaking her head.

"I'm sorry," Deb says softly. "The police and para-medics are on their way."

"Police?" Emmy demands. "What can the police do?"

"They have to attend all unexpected deaths," I explain.

"Death?" Emmy glares at me like I'm using a word in a foreign language. "He needs CPR!" She looks at Deb. "You know how to do CPR." Her eyes wide, she gestures toward Armando with her trembling hand. "Do it!"

Before Deb can respond to my sister's desperate plea, first responders fill the room.

"We're in the way," I whisper, tugging my sister's arm to coax her toward the door.

"I'm not leaving." Emmy yanks her arm away.

"Which one of you found him?" A uniformed police officer asks.

"Her."

"Me."

Emmy and I reply, both pointing at her.

"Oh, hi, Megan," the officer says. "Chief Sloane is on his way up."

"Thanks," I nod and attempt a small smile while trying to recall the officer's name.

By the time it occurs to me to look at the name badge on his uniform, he's leading my sister out of the bedroom. Unsure what to do, and wanting to stay out of the way, I slink out after them and join my sister on the sofa.

An authoritative, familiar voice protests the lack of light in the dim hotel suite. Eric.

A young police officer rushes to the window and combs through the pleats in the blackout curtains, searching for an opening. I stand up and wave Eric over just as the young officer opens the curtains and daylight pierces the room.

"What are you doing here?" he asks, rubbing my back. "Are you OK?" I nod. Eric scans the sofa, his gaze stopping on my sister. "Is Armando….?"

Squinting into the brightness, I nod and Eric curses under his breath. I look toward the bedroom and jerk my head. He nods and holds up an index finger.

"I'll be back," he says as he turns toward the bedroom.

The uniformed officer who accompanied my sister out of the bedroom is asking her questions. Her voice is quiet, and I can't hear her responses.

Deb is talking to a group of first responders. A police officer she's with nods and stands aside. She makes her way through the group to us.

"Let's go somewhere quieter," Deb suggests, taking my sister by the elbow. My sister opens her mouth to speak, but Deb speaks first and says, "I know you don't want to leave, but you'll be right next door."

"Megan's coming too?" Emmy asks, clenching a fistful of my rust-coloured cardigan.

"Of course," Deb replies, guiding us through the horde of moving uniforms.

Outside the room, we turn left and follow Deb down the corridor, single file, like ducklings waddling behind a mother duck, until she brings us to a stop. She swipes her keycard and holds the door while Emmy and I file past her into the vacant suite.

"Thanks, Deb." My voice hitches on her name, and I swallow an onslaught of tears.

Deb hugs me and her comforting embrace has the same intangible, maternal quality as Connie's, making it impossible to hold back the tears.

"If you need anything, text me," Deb says. I nod. She retrieves a box of tissues from the washroom and hands them to me. "Or pick up any landline and talk. The front desk knows you're here." I nod again. "I have to answer some questions for the police, but I'm not

59

leaving the building," she reassures me. Still trying to compose myself, I nod again. "Should I tell Connie?" Deb whispers as she reaches for the door handle.

"I'll let her know," I reply. "Thank you again."

After Deb leaves, I take a deep breath and blow it out. Then I take in my surroundings. This suite is the mirror image of Armando's suite, and except for a few minor differences, the decor is identical.

I collapse onto the sofa next to my sister and put the box of tissues on her lap. She uses one to dab her teary eyes and blow her nose.

"Do you want water or anything?" I ask.

She shakes her head.

"Do you want to lie down?"

She shakes her head, then looks me in the eye.

"My husband is dead, isn't he?"

I nod.

"I'm sorry, Emmy."

"How?" she asks, pulling a fresh tissue from the box and crying into it. "How? He's young. He's healthy. There weren't any marks on him. How?"

"I don't know," I say, hugging her while she cries into my shoulder.

While my sister cries on my shoulder and I try to make sense of her husband's sudden death, my phone dings, distracting me from my morbid ruminations.

"It's Dad," I say when I look at the screen.

Emmy jolts upright and tilts my phone so she can see the screen. I haven't opened the text message yet. The notification banner on the screen reads, *New Text Message From: Dad.*

"How did he find out?" Emmy asks, panicked. "Who told him?"

"He can't know," I say, thinking out loud. "It must be a coincidence."

"It has to be," Emmy agrees. She lifts her chin toward the screen. "Open it."

I unlock my phone and open the text message. It's a group message to me, Emmy, and Hannah.

"It's not about Armando," I say, looking at the text. "He sent us a photo of a grey-crested bird."

"Why?" Emmy asks.

I read her the text our Dad sent with the photo.

Dad: This is a Southern Lapwing, the national bird of Uruguay. He was wading in a puddle outside our window this morning.

"Uruguay?" Emmy asks. "I thought they were in Belize."

"I thought they were in Brazil," I add.

Hannah's response to the bird photo appears on the screen.

Hannah: Nice bird, Grandpa. I thought you were in Argentina? Followed by a bird emoji, a heart emoji, and the Argentinian flag emoji.

Dad: We're in Uruguay. Followed by the Uruguayan flag emoji.

"That's one mystery solved." I show Emmy our dad's text response to Hannah.

"When did Dad learn how to text photos?" Emmy wonders.

"The same day he learned how to use emojis?" I shrug.

"Do you want me to tell Dad and Zoe?" I ask.

"Not by text!" Emmy replies, appalled by the notion.

"I meant, should we phone them?"

"No." Emmy says, then she pauses while she thinks. "You know what they're like. They'll get on the next plane home. I can't deal with Zoe's chronic fussing or Dad's constant words of wisdom. And you know how he is, he'll make it about him. No, I don't want them here. Not yet."

Emmy's assessment of our dad and Zoe is pretty accurate. Our stepmum, Zoe, is a first-class fusser, even when the target of her fussing is less than enthusiastic. And our dad loves a captive audience. He thrives on being the centre of attention. I'd never say it to her face, but Emmy and our dad are similar; they're both charismatic and can command an audience.

"It would be awful if they find out from someone else," I say.

"Who would tell them?"

"Certain people have to know, Emmy. Like Armando's team, for example. And as soon as someone else knows, you can't control who they tell."

Emmy's eyes open wide and fill with panic and fear.

"People could already know." She stands up and paces in front of the sofa. "There were probably a dozen people in the other hotel room. It only takes one of them to recognize me or Armando for his death to be all over the internet. Or someone who works here might have disclosed it to someone."

"You think?" I ask, opening the web browser on my phone and typing Armando's name into the search bar.

"Well?" Emmy asks, still pacing and wringing her delicate hands. "Anything about Armando?"

"Nothing," I reply, not telling her about the article about their marital problems that I found on a gossip blog.

The article was posted early this morning. Before we found Armando's lifeless body. The headline reads, *Hello, divorce! You'll get a real kick out of this tidbit!* An obvious soccer pun and thinly veiled reference to my sister's morning show. Under the headline, the article continues:

Sources tell us a certain morning show co-host kicked her sporty husband off the marital pitch. Does she suspect foul play, or is their perfect match less perfect than everyone thinks? She said, Goodbye, work! and ran away from the game for a timeout with her family. He must be a soccer for her because he followed her. Will she decide he's a keeper or kick him to the curb?

The article doesn't mention Emmy and Armando by name, but the tacky soccer puns and implied references to Emmy's morning show make it obvious who the article is about. There's even a reference to the *Perfect Match* reality show, which is top secret until the network reveals the contestants. Who tipped them off? Only a handful of people know Emmy is in Harmony Lake, and even fewer know Armando followed her. Could the source be someone local? Someone I know or someone who works at the resort?

Luckily, the short, poorly written story hasn't been picked up by a more reputable website with a larger audience.

There's no need to share this with Emmy and cause her more distress, but I quickly copy the website address and text it to Eric. If Armando's death turns into a murder investigation, he might want to question the source of this nasty article.

"Let's phone Dad and Zoe," Emmy suggests. "Together. If I fall apart and can't talk, I'll need your help."

Before we phone them, we text Dad and Zoe and ask if they're available to talk. We don't want to break such shocking news to them while they're on a guided tour, or somewhere remote without the amenities they might need if one of them goes into shock, or reacts worse than expected.

CHAPTER 8

AFTER A TEARFUL, heartbreaking conversation with Dad and Zoe, we hang up. They took the news better than we expected but wanted to catch the next flight home. We dissuaded them by assuring them there won't be a funeral until after the coroner releases Armando's body. Emmy promised to call them every day, and we both promised to keep them up to date on the coroner's findings.

"I want to tell Poppy," Emmy says. "She's my best friend, and as my PA she'll arrange my bereavement leave with the network."

"Good idea," I agree.

"And I have to tell Brad Hendricks," she declares. "He'll know who to inform. Which sports people need to know. But I don't have my phone. I left it in my purse. In the other room."

I like that we're referring to the hotel room where Armando died as *the other hotel room*, or *the other room*.

The euphemisms are less distressing than *Armando's hotel room*, or *Armando's room.*

Someone knocks on the door, and I gesture for Emmy to sit down.

"Here." I thrust my phone toward her and stand up to answer the door. "Use my phone as long as you need. I'll use the landline to call April and Connie."

"Thanks, but I can't," she explains. "I store everyone's phone numbers in my phone. I don't have them memorized."

I peer through the peephole, and as if by divine intervention, Eric is standing in the hall, holding Emmy's purse.

"Your timing is perfect," I say when I open the door.

Eric kisses my forehead, and I step aside so he can come inside.

"I'm sorry I didn't get here sooner," he says. "The coroner arrived, and I couldn't get away. Are you OK?"

I nod.

"What did the coroner say?" Emmy jumps off the sofa and wrings her hands in front of her.

"He said he'll know more after the autopsy," Eric replies. "But there are no obvious signs of trauma or foul play."

Signs. When Eric says the word *signs*, I have a mental flashback to the DO NOT DISTURB sign Emmy removed from the door when we returned from brunch. I have to mention it to Eric, but not in front of Emmy. She has enough to deal with. The last thing she needs is me suggesting someone else was in Armando's room while we were at brunch.

"Does that mean Armando died of natural causes?" Emmy asks, her eyes pleading for the answer to be yes.

"It means we don't know for sure yet, but there's no reason to suspect it wasn't natural causes."

One of Eric's superpowers is answering a question without actually answering a question. It's frustrating as heck, and it's my least favourite superpower.

"Is my phone in there?" Emmy asks, pointing to her purse in Eric's hand.

"Yes." Eric looks at the purse in his hand like he's shocked it's there. "I had to go through it, but everything is in there," he says, handing her the designer handbag.

"Thank you." Emmy takes the purse and opens it, scans the contents, gives it a shake, then scans again, and pulls out her cell phone before closing it. "I need to notify Brad. Then I need to tell Poppy. Is it OK if I go in the next room?"

"Do you want me to come?" I offer.

"No, I'll be fine this time." She forces her mouth into a weak smile.

"I need to talk to you when you're finished," Eric says.

Emmy nods, then retreats to the bedroom, closing the door behind her.

"This time?" Eric asks, taking my hand and leading me to the sofa. "Who did Emmy already notify?"

"Dad and Zoe," I reply, then I tell him everything that happened, starting with when I arrived at Rise & Glide to pick up Emmy for brunch, and ending with his impeccable timing delivering Emmy's purse. I also mention the DO NOT DISTURB SIGN that was hanging on the door when we returned to the hotel.

"I'll have an officer take an inventory of the DO NOT DISTURB signs in Armando's room, and take them into evidence," Eric says, typing on his phone. "If there's only one sign, whoever hung it was in the room. And those signs are glossy, they hold fingerprints well."

"Also," I add, "I touched something in the bedroom."

I explain to Eric about my nausea and magnified senses, and that I touched the cloche because if I didn't cover the food on the room service cart, I would have thrown up.

"Are you feeling better now?" he asks, concerned.

"Yes," I assure him. "Physically, I'm fine. The situation overwhelmed me, and I freaked out."

Eric pulls me into him, and I rest my head and hand on his chest while he strokes my hair. I take a few deep breaths, and repeat the words, *heavy shoulders, long arms* in my head.

Heavy shoulders, long arms is a mantra I learned in a yoga class almost twenty years ago. It helps release the tension in my neck and shoulders.

"How are you emotionally?" Eric asks. "Do you need anything?"

"It's weird," I reply. "Armando was my brother-in-law, but we didn't know each other. They've been together for three years, but I've only met him a handful of times. I know our neighbours and even our postal carrier better than I knew Armando. I'm upset for Emmy, but not as upset as I'd expect, if that makes sense."

"Could be shock," Eric suggests. "Sometimes we suppress our feelings so we can function for someone else. You're taking care of Emmy right now. Maybe you'll have more feelings when she doesn't need you as much."

"Maybe," I agree but doubting it.

"Can I ask you a few questions about this morning?" Eric asks.

"Of course," I reply, sitting upright. "For Emmy's sake, I'll do whatever it takes to help get this over with."

"Was the food cart there when you picked up Emmy this morning?" Eric asks.

"I don't know." I shrug, shaking my head. "I didn't go into the bedroom when I picked her up. I was inside the suite for less than a minute. Emmy was ready when I arrived. She went into the bedroom to get her purse, then we left. The bedroom door was closed."

"So, you didn't *see* or *hear* Armando when you picked up Emmy?"

"That's right," I confirm. "Emmy said he was asleep." I tell him Emmy's joke about Armando being extra tired because they were up late *making up*. Recollecting the conversation reminds me of the resort employee we encountered. "He was pushing a room service cart down the hall. He said good morning to us. Maybe he was delivering the cart to Armando's room."

"Maybe," Eric says, making a note in his notebook. "I'm waiting for Deb to get me the access history to the room. The time when you picked up Emmy falls into the time window of when the coroner's estimates Armando died."

"The coroner thinks Armando could have died *before* Emmy and I left for brunch?" I ask, incredulous. "Eric, I think my sister would have noticed if her husband was dead."

He looks at me and places a hand on my knee. "The bedroom was dark, babe. You said she was in denial when he didn't talk to her. Deb said she was in denial and wanted her to attempt resuscitation."

He's right, but I just can't believe my sister could attend brunch and be her normal cheerful self, when she knew, even on a subconscious level, that her husband was dead.

"Does that happen?" I ask. "Do people fool themselves like that?"

"It could be an honest mistake. If he was dead, and I'm not saying he was, she might not have realized. She could have believed he was asleep. The room was pitch black."

"If the cart we saw in the hallway went to Armando's room, he couldn't have died before we left for brunch. If the food arrived after Emmy and I left, Armando was alive when I picked up my sister. He had to be."

"Because the food was partially eaten," Eric says, completing my thought. "He would've gotten out of bed, eaten, then returned to bed."

"Exactly! When you get the access records, we'll know who delivered the food to Armando and when they delivered it."

"And the coroner will confirm whether Armando ate the food on the tray, and approximately what time he ate it," Eric adds. "We took the food as evidence, in case it contributed to Armando's death."

Eric's phone rings. While he answers it, I crack open the bedroom door and peek inside. Emmy is sitting on the bed with her phone to her ear, used tissues piled into a small mountain on her lap. I step inside and close the door behind me.

"You OK?" I mouth when she looks at me.

Still holding the phone to her ear, she presses her lips into a tight line and nods.

"Do you need anything?" I ask silently, exaggerating each word so she can read my lips.

She shakes her head.

"I'm right outside," I whisper.

She nods again and mouths, "Thank you."

I leave the bedroom and return to the sitting area where Eric is ending his phone call.

"What's wrong?" I ask, when I see how tense his facial muscles are.

"Does Emmy smoke?"

"No."

"Was Armando a smoker?"

"Not that I'm aware of," I reply. "I meant to ask Emmy, but it didn't come up."

"Why would you ask Emmy if Armando was a smoker?"

"Same reason as you. The empty cigarette package

under the fern." I point to this hotel suite's almost-identical fern on an almost-identical round end table.

"There's a pack of cigarettes under the fern in Armando's room?" Eric asks, studying me with narrowed eyes.

I nod. "It was there when Emmy found Armando's body. Isn't that why you're asking if Armando smoked? Because of the cigarette packaging?"

"No," Eric replies. "I'm asking because we just found nicotine patches in Emmy's luggage."

"Why would Emmy have nicotine patches?"

What aren't you telling me, Emmy?

I sit on the sofa drumming my fingers and wishing I hadn't left my knitting in the car. I could use it right now to focus my worrying mind and occupy my idle hands. How will my sister explain the cigarette package in her hotel suite? And the nicotine patches in her luggage?

Eric is on the phone with an officer in Armando's suite, instructing them to confirm the cigarette package is still under the fern fronds and to collect it as evidence.

"Was it there?" I ask when he ends the call.

He nods. "Forensics will process it. They also found a few discarded cigarette butts in a bowl on the balcony. With any luck, they'll find DNA and fingerprints."

"I'm glad the package was still there."

"What package?" Emmy asks, emerging from the bedroom.

Her eyes are puffier and redder than before.

I look at Eric for guidance, and he gives me a discreet nod.

"The cigarette package near the fern in the other hotel room," I explain. "Did Armando smoke?"

If her answer is yes, this could open up some smoking-related, not-murder theories for how Armando died.

"No," Emmy says, bewildered. "What brand were they?"

"I'm not sure," I reply, wondering why the brand is relevant. "The room was kind of dark, and I'm not familiar with the different cigarette brands. The box was mostly white, if that helps."

"I've never seen Armando smoke, but he told me once that when he was younger—long before we met—he was a social smoker. When he went to clubs and stuff."

"I bet his trainers didn't like that," I comment.

"They didn't," Emmy concurs. "That's why he quit. He was afraid it would affect his performance on the pitch."

"Is it possible he started again?" Eric asks.

Panic flashes in Emmy's eyes, and she gasps, bringing her hand to her mouth.

"Oh my god! I killed my husband!"

CHAPTER 9

I RUSH OVER to Emmy and slap my hand over her mouth.

Alarmed and confused, she digs her fingers between my hand and her face and tries to wrench my hand away. I push her hand down, and she stops struggling. She looks at me, terrified. What's wrong with her eyes? Why do they look like that? *Focus, Megan.*

"Don't say another word!" I command. "Emmy, I mean it. Don't talk."

I look at her, searching for agreement. She nods, and the muscles around her eyes relax. Scrutinizing her expression, I realize why her eyes look strange.

"I'm going to remove my hand. Say nothing." She nods again. I remove my hand, and my sister locks eyes with me. "Repeat after me," I instruct. "I want my lawyer."

Emmy opens her mouth to protest, or question me, or something, but I shoot her a stern glare that lets her know, in no uncertain terms, I'm dead serious. Pardon the pun.

"I want my lawyer," Emmy mumbles, our gazes still locked.

"Tell him," I whisper, pointing at Eric.

The confusion that clouds her face is replaced by comprehension, and Emmy turns to Eric, straightening her spine.

"I won't say anything else or answer questions without my lawyer present."

"Understood," Eric replies.

I blow out a sigh of relief.

"You're missing a contact lens," I say to Emmy, pointing to her left eye, which is its natural hazel colour. Her right eye is still the emerald green I've grown accustomed to. "You must have cried it out."

"I should take out the other one," she says. "I'll be right back."

"Why did you muzzle her like that?" Eric asks after the bedroom door closes.

"Because you're a cop," I reply. "You already suspect Armando died before Emmy left the hotel this morning. Which means if Armando was murdered, you think Emmy is a suspect. I had to stop her before she said something else self-incriminating in front of you."

He looks at me speechless, and his eyes are sad, like a wounded animal.

"Honey, I'm sorry." I take his hand. "You know what Emmy is like. Sometimes she speaks before she thinks. Like a minute ago when she accused herself of killing Armando."

"You mean when she *confessed* to killing Armando," he corrects me.

"It wasn't a confession, Eric, and you know it. It was a spontaneous outburst from an overwhelmed, traumatized widow, who's trying to survive the worst day of her life."

"You're good," he says with a chuckle, "but I can't pretend she didn't say it."

"I know." I nod. "That's why I stopped her before she said something else."

I unlock my phone and open the messaging app, my thumbs darting back and forth across the keyboard.

Me: Emmy needs a lawyer. It's urgent.

"Who are you texting?" Eric asks.

"Emmy's lawyer," I reply, hitting send.

"Adam?" he asks. "You're inviting your ex-husband to this family crisis and freezing me out?" The pain in his voice makes my heart ache.

"Honey, I'm sorry. But you're a cop," I reiterate. "And I'm not inviting my ex-husband, I'm contacting my sister's lawyer. They just happen to be the same person."

"I'm your fiancé and Emmy's future brother-in-law," Eric reminds me, his voice sad and quiet.

"You're also the chief of police," I counter. "In this situation, how can you be both?" I ask rhetorically. "I'm sorry, Eric. My sister is having the worst day of her life, and she needs me right now. I have to protect her."

My phone dings.

Adam: Where?

"Adam?" Eric asks.

"Uh-huh." I nod, typing a response to Adam.

Me: Rise & Glide. Room 808.

Adam: On my way. Try to keep her quiet until I get there.

Adam gets it. He knows Emmy needs guidance and support from a voice of reason.

"I can't believe how swollen and blotchy my eyes are," Emmy says, using one hand to feel her way out of the bedroom, while her other hand presses a cold, damp washcloth against her eyes. "Eric," she says, facing the wrong direction.

"Over here, Emmy," he responds.

Following the sound of his voice, she turns her head and almost faces him.

"May I go back to the other room?" she asks. "I need my hemorrhoid cream." She turns away from me. "Megan, do you know if I remembered to pack my hemorrhoid cream? Did you see it when I stayed at your place?"

I shake my head out of habit, then realize she can't see me because she's facing away from me, and the washcloth is covering her eyes.

"I don't know," I say.

"The other room is a crime scene until the coroner determines how Armando died," Eric explains. "I can't let anyone access it."

"Can someone bring me the hemorrhoid cream?"

"I'm afraid not," Eric replies.

"There might be ice in the ice bucket," I suggest.

"You could make an ice pack. Maybe you should lie down and rest your eyes."

Emmy nods. "I don't want to leave until the swelling goes down. What if someone takes my picture and posts it online?"

Emmy gropes her way back to the bedroom and closes the door behind her.

"What was that about?" Eric asks.

"Because of her job, Emmy is vigilant about her appearance when she's out in public," I reply. "I don't blame her. I wouldn't want my photo posted online if I were crying, and I'm not a public figure."

"No, I mean the hemorrhoid cream," Eric clarifies. "Why does she want hemorrhoid cream for her eyes?"

"It reduces swelling," I explain.

"Eww," Eric cringes, scrunching his nose.

"She doesn't use it anywhere else," I assure him. "And if she did, each body part would have a separate tube."

"That makes sense," he says, less repulsed by the idea of using cream intended for one body part on another. "Listen, babe, I'm sorry I got defensive when you stopped your sister from talking, and when you texted Adam for her. I overreacted. I want to support you and Emmy, not investigate the situation. The coroner hasn't declared Armando's death a murder yet..."

"Hold that thought," I say, interrupting Eric's apology when someone knocks on the door.

Adam must have been nearby when I texted him,

otherwise he just set a land speed record getting here from his condo.

"I'll go," Eric says when I motion to stand up.

While Eric answers the door, I reflect on what he said. He said, *the coroner hasn't declared Armando's death a murder yet.* Yet. He might not want to admit it, but Eric thinks Armando was murdered, and he expects the coroner to reach the same conclusion.

Whoever knocked on the door, it isn't Adam. But his voice is familiar. I've heard it before but can't place it. It's probably a police officer from the other hotel room.

Frustrated that I can't connect the familiar voice to its owner, I stand up and crane my neck to see who it is.

"Brad?"

"Megan?"

"What are you doing here?"

"Emmy called and told me about Armando. I came to see her."

Eric moves aside, permitting Brad access to the hotel suite. As soon as he's within six feet of me, I smell it. Cigarettes. Either Brad is a smoker, or he was just with someone who smokes.

"Emmy told you what room we're in?"

"No, I asked the front desk. The hotel knows Armando and I arrived together. I booked both suites in my name. I'm staying down the hall."

"Armando didn't mention that you're in town too."

I think back to Friday when Armando visited me at Knitorious. He said Brad booked his suite, but I don't remember him saying anything about Brad accompanying him to Harmony Lake.

"I tagged along for moral support," Brad explains. "Armando was pretty worried. He and Emmy had a huge argument. Armando thought she was serious when she threatened to divorce him. I came with him in case his attempt to win her back didn't go well."

"It's nice to see you again," I say. "I'm sorry it's under such awful circumstances."

"Same here," Brad says, then we share an awkward hug that convinces me Brad is a smoker. "You look great, by the way. Divorce agrees with you."

"Thank you?" I'm not sure how to respond to his odd compliment. "You met Eric at the door, I presume?"

I gesture to Eric, who extends his hand for Brad to shake.

"Yeah, you said you're the police chief?" Brad asks, shaking hands with Eric. "Why is the police chief here if Armando died in his sleep?"

Emmy told Brad that Armando died in his sleep? But we don't know if that's true. I guess she had to tell him something when he asked.

"We attend all unexpected deaths," Eric explains.

"And we're engaged," I add. "Eric is my fiancé."

"Oh." Shocked, Brad looks from me to Eric, back to me, then at my engagement ring. "Armando never mentioned it. Congratulations."

"Thanks," Eric and I respond.

Aside from Emmy and Armando's reception after they eloped, I've only met Brad twice before today. He's a sports agent and former athlete. He looks like a former athlete. Not that all former athlete's look the same, but if you drew a caricature of a former athlete, I'm betting it would resemble Brad. He looks like a middle-aged version of every jock I went to school with. He's tall, fit, has perfect posture, short hair, perfect teeth, and a deep voice. This is our third encounter, and the third time I've seen him wear a collared golf shirt and khaki golf pants.

"Emmy was so upset she could barely talk when she called me," Brad says. "I didn't want to make it worse, so I didn't ask her anything. But I need to know. What happened? How could Armando die in his sleep? I was with him yesterday, and he looked great. There was nothing wrong with him."

"He died in bed," I clarify. "We don't know if he died in his sleep."

"What do we know?" Brad asks, looking back and forth between me and Eric.

"We're waiting for the coroner to establish how Armando died. In the meantime, we treat it like a crime scene," Eric says.

"A crime scene?" Brad asks, awestruck. "Armando was a strong, fit guy. If he saw it coming, he would've put up a fight. Did he put up a fight?"

"Have a seat, Brad," Eric urges. "I need to ask you a few questions."

"Armando was with Emmy most of yesterday and all night. If something happened to him, she either did it or knows who did," Brad accuses.

"Whoa!" I say, offended on my sister's behalf.

"What's going on out here?" Emmy says from the bedroom doorway. "Brad? What are you doing here?"

"Looking for answers," Brad replies. "You called and told me my best friend died but didn't give me any details or an explanation. I need to know what happened to Armando."

"I wasn't keeping anything from you, Brad. I don't have any details or an explanation." Emmy's eyes well up with fresh tears. "We don't know yet how he died."

"C'mon, Emmy," Brad chortles. "You were alone with him all night. Tell us what happened. What did you do?"

"Hey!" Eric positions himself in front of Brad, blocking his view of Emmy. "Enough! Let's talk at the station."

"Are you serious?" Brad asks. "Why are you taking me to the station? Take her. She's the one hiding something."

"Let's go." Eric escorts Brad to the door, and they leave.

"I see why you think Brad doesn't like you," I say to my sister when we're alone.

"He doesn't even try to hide it," Emmy responds.

"You haven't eaten since brunch. That was hours ago. You should eat something."

"I won't be able to keep it down, Sis." She looks at me. "Do you think Armando is still in the other room?"

I shake my head. "The body usually leaves with the coroner. Anyway, if Armando is there, they won't let you see him."

"I know," Emmy says. "I don't want to leave the hotel before him. I don't want him to be alone. Is that weird?"

"No, it's not weird. Nothing you feel right now is weird." I squeeze her hand. "Adam is on his way, as your lawyer. After you talk to him, I'll ask Eric if I can take you home."

"And you'll make sure Armando leaves first?"

I nod.

CHAPTER 10

EMMY and I sit in exhausted silence, waiting for Adam to arrive when her phone rings.

"It's the head of the network," she says, looking at her phone screen.

"You don't have to answer it," I remind her.

"No, I'll take it," she decides, then puts the phone to her ear and does a decent impersonation of a cheerful hello.

I only overhear some of their conversation before Emmy disappears into the bedroom and closes the door, but it sounds like the caller is offering condolences on behalf of the network that airs *Hello, today!*. They must have heard about Armando's death from Poppy. News of Armando's death is reaching more and more people, and I'm worried the unavoidable onslaught of attention will overwhelm Emmy.

While Emmy is on the phone with the network executive, I call April and Connie to tell them what happened. I don't want my best friends to hear it through the rumour mill.

"We can be home by tonight if we pack and leave now," April says.

She's shuffling things in the background. Is she already packing?

"No," I insist. "Stay with your family. Armando's death is a reminder that anything can happen at any time. You should spend as much time enjoying your family as possible. Emmy won't want Armando's death to cast a shadow over your cousin's wedding celebration. Please stay. You'll be home on Friday, anyway."

It takes some more convincing, but April agrees to stay put. I agree to contact her right away if I change my mind and want her to come home.

Connie, who's amazing in a crisis, jumps into action and is on her way to my house to pick up Sophie. It's a relief to stop worrying about Sophie's routine of scheduled walks and meals.

"I have to go, Connie. I think Adam's here."

A second knock on the door. With the phone to my ear, I open it and beckon Adam inside.

"Keep me up to date," Connie instructs. "I'm just pulling into your driveway. Don't worry about Sophie. We'll keep her as long as you need."

I thank Connie, and we end the call.

"What's going on, Meg?" Adam demands. "The elevators won't stop on this floor without a special key, and there are police officers in the stairwell, preventing people from accessing the eighth floor."

"How did you get up here?"

"I texted Eric, and he sent a cop to accompany me."

"I didn't know any of that was happening," I tell him. "Emmy and I haven't left this hotel suite since we left your place after brunch."

"Why?"

I guide Adam to the seating area, and we sit down.

"Armando's dead."

"What? How? When?"

"I don't know," I reply, frustrated by the lack of answers.

I tell Adam everything that has happened since Emmy and I left his condo after brunch, then I wait while he considers what he just heard.

"Did you tell Hannah?" he asks after he processes the deluge of facts and details I flooded him with.

"Not yet. I want to talk to her without rushing. I thought I'd call her when Emmy goes to sleep."

"I'd like to be there," Adam says.

"Of course," I agree. "I assumed you would."

"Poor Emmy!" Adam says with a heavy sigh. "Where is she?"

"In the bedroom talking on the phone. First the network phoned her, then Poppy phoned her again. She's overwhelmed, Adam. She's functioning, but I don't know if the reality has hit her yet, if that makes sense."

Adam nods. "Can I do anything? Other than as her lawyer. As family. What can I do?"

"I don't know." I shrug.

"I knew I heard voices," Emmy says when she opens the bedroom door.

"Emmy, I'm so sorry to hear about Armando."

Adam stands up, and Emmy crumples into his arms, sobbing.

While Emmy soaks Adam's chest with tears, I search the bedroom and both washrooms for more tissues. Nothing. We've used them all. I pick up the landline and request more tissues from the front desk, then bring Emmy a roll of toilet paper to dry her tears. For whatever reason, the toilet paper amuses her, and she goes from tears of grief to tears of laughter. Emotions are weird.

By the time Emmy composes herself, Deb Kee restocks the suite with several boxes of tissues and encourages us to eat by bringing us refreshments. She took it upon herself to bring us coffee, tea, juice, a fruit platter, a cheese and cracker tray, and a variety of finger sandwiches.

"Just have a bite," I coax Emmy. "One cracker? A piece of cheese? One strawberry?"

Emmy crinkles her nose and shakes her head. She pushes away the plate I made her.

"I can't. Maybe later."

"OK," I say, returning the plate to the room service cart. "You have to drink some water, though." I nudge the glass toward her.

"Fine," she agrees to shut me up.

With all the crying, I'm worried Emmy will get dehydrated if she doesn't drink enough. None of us have an appetite. Food seems so complicated and unappealing right now.

"When you're ready, Emmy, I need you to tell me everything," Adam says.

Emmy nods, then tells Adam what she remembers since we left him after brunch. Her version of events is almost identical to mine. Under the circumstances, her recollection is more lucid and detailed than I expect. She also tells us some intimate details about her relationship with Armando that I wasn't aware of until now. After her disclosure, I understand why my sister accused herself of killing Armando when Eric and I asked her about the cigarette package we found in the other hotel room.

Emmy's mouth and throat are dry after all the talking, and she drinks an entire glass of water. Success! As I refill her glass, someone knocks on the door.

"It's Eric," I say, peeping through the peephole.

Eric walks over to Emmy and hands her a small bag from the local pharmacy.

"Hemorrhoid cream," he says. "I wasn't sure which brand to get. There are a few different ones."

"Thank you, that's thoughtful. Something Armando would do," Emmy says, standing up to hug him. "I'll be right back." She excuses herself and disappears into the bedroom with the pharmacy bag.

I'm dying to ask Eric what Brad said at the station. But Emmy will be back any second, and I'm not sure he can talk about it in front of Emmy's lawyer.

"Do you think she can handle a few questions?" Eric asks, looking back and forth from me to Adam.

"She wants to cooperate," Adam says in his lawyer voice. "If she can't cope, I'll end the interview."

Eric nods and sits down.

I go into the bedroom to check on Emmy. She's in the washroom, assessing her eyes in the mirror.

"Do you still want to talk to Eric?" I ask.

She nods, looking at me in the mirror. "I want to help. I want the coroner to determine that Armando died of natural causes, and I want Eric to close the file."

We return from the bedroom, and Adam shoots Emmy a look. She nods, then he nods.

"Emmy, tell Eric everything you told me," Adam says.

"All of it?" Emmy asks, shifting uncomfortably next to me on the sofa.

"All of it," Adam confirms.

While Eric jots down notes in his notebook, Emmy tells him everything that happened from the time she woke up this morning until he brought her purse from the other hotel room to this one.

Eric asks Emmy some clarifying questions about her version of events, and so far, Emmy is holding herself together, and the interview is going well.

"Was the room service cart in the room when you left for brunch?" Eric asks.

"No," Emmy replies. "It wasn't there. And my husband was alive. We said good morning. I kissed him goodbye before I left, and he kissed me back."

This means Armando was alive when we left for brunch. He was alive to open the door for the food, and he was alive to eat it. I knew Emmy didn't kill him.

"Who hung the DO NOT DISTURB sign on the door?"

Taken aback, Emmy looks to the side and small creases fight through the Botox and appear between her eyes.

"I don't know," she replies. "Now that you mention it, I remember taking the DO NOT DISTURB sign off the door, but I don't remember Armando hanging it up. We never use the DO NOT DISTURB sign in hotels because we always decline housekeeping when we check in."

Eric nods and makes notes in his notebook.

"Do you want to tell me anything else?" he asks.

Emmy looks at Adam, and he nods.

"There's one more thing." Emmy takes a deep breath and pulls herself to her full seated height.

"Brace yourself," I whisper to Eric with my eyebrows raised.

Panic flashes across his face as he tries to guess what kind of intimate information he should prepare himself to hear about his future sister-in-law.

"Armando travels a lot." Emmy begins by providing some background information that gives important context to the rest of her story. "Like, a lot. He's away— he was away—more than half the year, and I can't travel with him because my job keeps me at home from Monday to Friday, and I do appearances on weekends. Anyway," Emmy refocuses, "when Armando and I were in the same bed, I had this... thing... I would do to him."

Eric shifts in his chair and swallows hard. I try not to smile at his discomfort.

"I'm listening," he says, then inhales deeply and blows it out.

"When we went to bed, I would wait for Armando to fall asleep. It never took long, Armando is—was—a great sleeper. Then, I would very carefully stick a nicotine patch on him. In the morning, I'd wake up before him—also easy since my body is used to waking up at 4 a.m. every day for work—and carefully remove the patch without waking him. I'd hide the patch by wrapping it in toilet paper and placing it at the bottom of the garbage pail." Emmy shrugs. "He was none the wiser."

Eric looks at me, confused.

"Is this another strange beauty trick like the hemorrhoid cream?"

"No," I reply. "It's a trick, but not the beauty kind."

"It had nothing to do with beauty," Emmy explains. "After a few nights of sleeping with the nicotine patch, Armando became... dependent on them.

"You mean addicted," Eric corrects her. "Did Armando know you were drugging him with nicotine while he slept?"

"Of course not," Emmy replies. "That would defeat the purpose."

"What purpose?" Eric asks, squeezing his brows together. "Why would you drug your husband without his consent?"

"When he'd go back on the road, he'd have trouble sleeping. Armando didn't know it was because of nicotine withdrawal. He thought he couldn't sleep without me." She looks down at her hands and wrings them in her lap. "It made him miss me when we were apart," she adds, still staring at her wringing hands and avoiding eye contact with Eric.

"And when Megan found the cigarette package, you assumed it was Armando's, and you panicked," Eric deduces. "It's dangerous to use a nicotine patch and smoke. It can cause heart problems. You thought the patch and your manipulative scheme killed him."

Emmy nods then launches into a fresh round of sobs and fights to collect herself so she can continue.

"It seemed harmless when I did it," Emmy explains between sobs. "It didn't occur to me that Armando was a former smoker, and the patches might give him cravings. Also, Brad smokes, so besides the patches, Armando was inhaling secondhand smoke from Brad. When you guys asked me about the cigarette package, I panicked. What if Armando started smoking again to satisfy his nicotine cravings? What if he was smoking in secret and didn't tell me? I put a nicotine patch on him last night, Eric. If my husband died of a heart attack, it's my fault."

CHAPTER 11

EMMY AND I CAN LEAVE. Finally. It's only been one afternoon, but it feels like we've been trapped in this luxury hotel suite for weeks. I can't wait to change into comfy clothes and relax in my not-luxurious-but-comfortable home. But Emmy refuses to leave. Her eyes are still swollen, and her sunglasses are in the other hotel room.

"Take mine," I insist, thrusting them toward her. "I have a backup pair in the car."

"It's not just the sunglasses, sis. I don't have any of my stuff. I can't change my clothes or even have a shower."

Emmy crosses her arms in front of her and huffs. I sympathize. She's lost her husband, and everything she owns is down the hall yet inaccessible to her. I'd hate to be in her position.

"You can borrow anything I own. Anything at all. We'll get you settled at home, then make a list of what you need, and I'll get it."

I'm sure Connie will stay with Emmy while I pick up provisions.

"I'm doing everything I can to get you access to your belongings as soon as possible," Eric promises.

"Where's Armando?" Emmy asks, looking at Eric with pleading, desperate eyes.

"He's at the morgue," Eric explains. "The coroner will conduct a post-mortem, then release the body. When the coroner releases Armando's body, you can arrange for whichever funeral home you choose to pick him up."

Judging by the expression on Emmy's face, this information overwhelms her.

"Not today," I assure her. "You don't have to decide yet. It'll be a few days at least."

"Good," Emmy mumbles. "I don't know any funeral homes."

"Emmy, this is all standard procedure," Adam adds, using his reassuring, non-lawyer voice. "In fact, Eric has made a few exceptions for you. He should have separated you and Meg until after you were both questioned. But he let you stay together. Alone. Without a police chaperone."

Emmy nods, crying silently.

Adam's right. Eric broke the rules for us. And if Armando was murdered, this special treatment could compromise the case. His career and reputation could be on the line. Guilt washes over me for not once considering the fine line Eric has to walk between being an excellent investigator and a supportive fiancé and future brother-in-law.

"I'll walk you out," I say to Adam.

"I'll get someone to bring you the elevator," Eric adds. "It won't stop on this floor without a key."

"It's fine," Adam says. "I'll take the stairs. It'll be good for me," he chuckles and rubs his flat stomach.

He's trying to lighten the mood. Adam is as lean today as he was the day we met when I was eighteen, and he knows it. He's proud and often brags about his superpower of eating whatever he wants and still fitting into clothes he wore twenty years ago.

"Thank you for... for... everything," I say to Adam as we walk to the door that leads to the staircase. "I don't know what we would've done without you today. Emmy listens to you more than anyone else."

"You don't have to thank me, Meg. I love Emmy like a sister. I'd do anything for either of you." He stops walking, so I stop. He turns to me. "I'll do anything to help. I know I wasn't always there for you. I might have let you down in marriage, but I won't let you down in divorce."

"Ditto," I blurt out, welling up with tears. "I'm sorry," I say, apologizing for my emotional collapse. "It's been a long, horrible day."

"You're doing great," Adam says, hugging me. "Emmy will be fine. Eventually. Until then, everyone wants to help."

I wipe my eyes and resume walking to the stairs.

"We should tell Hannah soon," Adam says. "Before she hears it from someone else."

"I know," I agree as we stop at the door to the stairwell and smile at the police officer standing guard.

"Meet me at the house. Let yourself in. I'll get Emmy settled, then we'll call Hannah."

THE DRIVE HOME IS QUIET. Emmy cries silent tears and stares out the window, watching the world pass.

"It was nice of Deb to let us leave through the delivery entrance," I say to break the silence.

"Yes, it was," Emmy agrees. "She was great. I'll have to send her a thank you gift and a note."

"I'll take care of it," I offer, relieved to do something useful.

When she heard about Emmy's concern that someone might recognize or photograph her leaving the hotel, Deb sprang into action and drove my car around to the delivery entrance behind the kitchen. Then, assuring us there would be no video surveillance cameras, she led us down the hall, to the room next door to the room where Armando died. Though it looked like just another hotel room door, it led to a maze of employee-only service hallways. Deb navigated us through them and escorted us downstairs on a service elevator. We slipped out of the hotel and into my waiting car unseen by anyone aside from a handful of kitchen employees, delivery people, and employees who were having their break outside near the delivery dock. Deb assured us all staff members sign a confidentiality agreement as a condition of employment. Any employee who discloses information about Emmy or Armando would lose their job.

"Whose car is that?" I ask, pulling over on the street outside my house. "I recognize Adam's car, but I don't recognize the other one."

"It's Poppy's rental car," Emmy says, unbuckling her seatbelt.

"Poppy? Didn't you talk to her on the phone earlier? How did she get to Harmony Lake so fast?"

"She got here this morning," Emmy explains. "I phoned her yesterday to tell her Armando and I were working things out. I told her I plan to stay in town until after Thanksgiving, so I could have Thanksgiving with my family. Poppy and I always have Thanksgiving together. I didn't want to leave her on her own, so I invited her to come to Harmony Lake for Thanksgiving too. I hope you don't mind."

"Of course, I don't mind," I insist. "The more the merrier." I wince as soon as my ears hear the insensitive comment my mouth blurts out. "I don't mean Thanksgiving will be merry. I mean, I haven't seen Poppy in ages. Also, you need your best friend right now, so I'm glad she's here for you."

It's quite a coincidence that Poppy is already in town when Emmy needs her more than ever. And she showed up for Thanksgiving a week early? On such brief notice? Did Poppy arrive in town before or after Armando died? My intuition tells me Poppy's timing is more than a coincidence.

"Emmy!"

Poppy and Emmy throw their arms around each other and cry into each other's shoulders.

"Hi, Poppy," I say. "We're glad you're here."

97

"Where else would I be?" Poppy asks, freeing up an arm to fold me into a group hug with her and Emmy. "I can't believe it. I'm still in shock."

"We're all in shock," Emmy mutters, pulling away from our embrace. "I need to freshen up."

"Use anything of mine you want," I insist, spying Adam waiting in the living room. "Poppy, can you help Emmy get settled and find whatever she needs? Adam and I need to call Hannah."

"Of course," Poppy replies, draping a protective arm around Emmy's shoulder.

"Emmy knows where everything is," I say. "If you need me, just shout."

Nodding, Poppy guides my sister toward the bedrooms, mumbling comforting words as they go.

"She was in the driveway when I got here," Adam explains, referring to Poppy.

"Thank you for letting her in."

"I sent Hannah a text while the three of you were hugging," Adam continues. "I asked if she could talk. She knows something's up. I told her we want to talk to her together."

"OK." I nod in agreement, dreading the conversation we're about to have with our daughter.

"How's Emmy?" I ask when Poppy appears in the kitchen alone.

"Better than I expected," Poppy replies. "She showered and put on your white pajamas. I laid with her until she fell asleep."

"Thank you," I say, hugging Poppy and squeezing her tight. "I can't believe how good your timing is. You appeared in my driveway right when Emmy needs you most."

"It's not a coincidence," Poppy says, taking a seat at the kitchen table. "I left for Harmony Lake yesterday when Emmy told me Brad was here. I figured he'd try to cause trouble, and Emmy might need me. I travelled all night. When I got here early this morning, I was exhausted, so I checked into that little motel off the highway. When I woke up, I phoned Emmy to let her know I was here. She was at brunch with you and Adam. She said she'd call me after you dropped her off at the hotel. Next thing I know, she called and told me Armando was dead. I couldn't believe it. He was fine when she left, then dead when she got back. How does that happen?"

Poppy asks the same question we're all asking.

I offer Poppy a coffee, and she accepts. Even though it's late in the day, I decide to join her and take out two pods of hazelnut cream. Time has no meaning today; we're all doing whatever it takes to get through each torturous moment.

"Why did you follow Brad here?"

"I don't trust Brad Hendricks as far as I can throw him," Poppy reveals. "He hates Emmy. She wanted Armando to fire Brad and sign with a better agent. I'm sure he came to Harmony Lake with Armando to stop them from working things out."

"Because if Emmy and Armando worked it out, it would mean Brad would lose a client," I conclude.

"Exactly," Poppy concurs.

"Brad told me he tagged along to offer Armando moral support."

"Ha!" Poppy blurts, her chestnut brown ponytail bouncing. Then, she smiles for the first time today, and her single dimple winks at me. "The only person Brad Hendricks wants to support is himself. He knows Emmy was serious about leaving Armando. If Armando didn't agree to fire Brad and sign with another agent, she was out."

I wonder if Brad knows Armando agreed to fire him to save his marriage?

"Emmy can't access her belongings for a few days," I explain. "I told her I'd get whatever necessities she needs until then."

"I can make a list for you," Poppy offers. "I know which brands to get, and which stores sell them, and everything."

I place a pen and some paper in front of Poppy.

"That would be awesome. Thank you, Poppy. Can you stay with Emmy while I get everything on the list? I don't want to leave her alone."

"Why don't I go?" Poppy suggests. "It'll be easier. I know what to get. And I know what to substitute if necessary."

"Thank you." I force a tight smile. "You know my sister better than I do."

"She's my best friend and my boss," Poppy chuckles.

"Is knowing what toiletries she prefers a best-friend duty or a PA duty?"

"Both," she replies without looking up from the list she's making.

"Is part of your job as Emmy's PA to monitor the internet for posts and stories about her?"

"Yes," Poppy replies, putting down the pen and looking at me. "I have alerts set up with her name and nickname. I get a notification whenever a new link mentions her."

"Did you see this?" I unlock my phone and open the web browser, then find the gossip site's implied post about Emmy and Armando's marriage, and hand my phone to Poppy.

"I haven't seen it," Poppy confirms, shaking her head. "I didn't get a notification because the post doesn't mention her name. It's a low blow, but Emmy's used to gossip sites writing crap about her. Sadly, it comes with the territory when you're on TV." She hands the phone back to me. "Did Emmy see this?"

"I don't think so," I reply. "I'll tell her how I found the post by accident while searching for information about Armando because Emmy's worried someone might have leaked his death."

"Can you send me the link?" Poppy asks. "I'll use the contact link at the bottom of the page to contact them and ask them to remove it. I don't know if they will, but I can ask."

"I'm sure the police will ask them to remove it too," I comment, texting the link to Poppy.

"Police?" Poppy asks, concerned. "Why do the

police care? Gossip sites post fake stories about celebrities all the time."

"But this isn't fake," I point out. "Whoever tipped off the gossip site has inside information about Emmy and Armando's marriage and their whereabouts. There's even a reference to *Perfect Match*. If someone murdered Armando, the police will want to know who wrote this and why."

"Murder?" Poppy's brown eyes are wide. "Emmy said Armando died in bed."

"He did," I confirm. "But *how* he died is still a mystery. The police have to treat it like a crime until the coroner confirms otherwise."

"Oh. I didn't know." Poppy's face droops. "Poor Emmy." She looks at me. "She's waiting to find out if someone murdered her husband."

CHAPTER 12

"Do you think someone killed Armando?" April's voice asks in my Airpods as I ease my car into the garage.

Since Adam left in his car to go home, and Poppy left in her car to get Emmy's necessities, I can move my car off the street. I pull it into the garage, so the driveway will be available for Eric and whoever else might need to park at our house today.

"I don't know," I admit. "But I think Eric suspects murder."

"Why?" April asks.

"A slip of the tongue," I reply. "He said the coroner hasn't determined if it's murder *yet*. As in, he expects the coroner will determine that Armando was murdered."

"I hate to say it, but my first thought was murder too."

"Me too," I admit with a sigh. "How else do you

justify a young, healthy person dying suddenly with no signs of trauma and no evidence of an accident?"

"I hope we're wrong," April says. "I hope Armando died of natural causes."

While April and I discuss how strange it feels to hope for a specific cause of death, another unfamiliar car pulls into the driveway.

"Who's this?" I wonder out loud.

"Who's who?" April asks. "Is someone there? I can't see, remember? I'm four hours away at my aunt's house."

The car's occupant gets out, sees me in the garage, and waves. His upper body disappears inside the car, and he re-emerges with flowers.

"Hi, Rich," I call out, waving over my head.

"Rich Kendall?" April whispers in my ear as if he can hear her.

"Yup," I whisper. "In the flesh."

"Holy guacamole, Megapop, did your sister's friends and coworkers charter a bus to follow her to Harmony Lake? Rich is the third person to follow her."

"Fourth," I correct her. "Armando, Brad, Poppy, and now Rich. It's strange. I have to go. I'll call you back."

I tap my Airpod to end the call and join Rich on the driveway, giving him a hug.

"Megan," Rich says, smiling, yet still sad. "It's lovely to see you again. Too bad it has to be under such sad circumstances."

Obviously, Rich has heard about Armando.

"Yes, it's been an awful day," I agree. "Let's talk inside."

On Emmy's behalf, I thank Rich for the flowers and take them from him.

"Flowers seem like such a trite offering for such a significant shock, but I didn't know what else to do." Rich smooths his sandy blond hair, ensuring his side part is tidy and tugs the sleeves of his pullover, exposing blond-haired forearms. "I was hoping to see Emmy," Rich says, easing himself onto the living room sofa. "Is she here?"

"She's asleep," I reply. "I'd rather not wake her." I place the flowers on the coffee table and straighten a few blooms that shifted in transit.

"Of course," Rich agrees. "Let her rest."

"Does Emmy know you're in town?"

"I don't think so," Rich confesses. "*I* didn't know I was coming. It was a spontaneous decision."

"A flight followed by a long drive was spontaneous?" I ask.

Rich chuckles but ignores my question.

"I got here last night, checked into my room, and lost my nerve. I was going to leave town today, and Emmy would've never known I was here. But when Poppy called and told me about Armando, I couldn't leave."

"What do you mean, you lost your nerve? Why did you come to Harmony Lake?"

"I know what happened between Emmy and Armando," Rich divulges. "I know the network offered them a spot on *Perfect Match*."

This doesn't answer my question. What did Rich plan to do before he lost his nerve?

"Did Emmy confide in you?" I ask.

Besides having crazy-good chemistry on screen, Emmy and Rich are friends off screen too. But I didn't know Emmy confides in him about her marriage.

I've always suspected Rich is in love with Emmy, or at least has a crush on her. I've never mentioned it to her, and I don't know if I'm right. I have nothing to base my suspicion on other than the way he looks at her. Rich Kendall looks at my sister the same way I look at a skein of half-price cashmere yarn in my favourite colour. Also, in a crowded room, every time I'd glance at Rich, I'd catch him watching Emmy with the same smitten expression Eric has when I catch him watching me in a crowded room.

"Of course, she told me," Rich replies. "We're friends. Friends tell each other things. Also, Emmy's appearance on *Perfect Match* would impact me. I'd either be without a co-host on *Hello, today!* or the network would have to arrange a roster of rotating co-hosts."

"Right," I say. "I didn't think of that."

"Emmy was so excited, she couldn't wait to tell me. When Armando said no, she was devastated. Their marriage wasn't easy. They hardly ever saw each other. And when they were together, she didn't fit into his disciplined life. Sometimes Emmy felt like she was an inconvenience Armando had to fit in between the demands of his team and his health regime."

"Wow," I say, shocked.

I offer Rich a refreshment, and he accepts a glass of water. I excuse myself, go to the kitchen to get his water, and process the revelation Rich just told me about Emmy's marriage.

This is the first I've heard that Emmy and Armando were anything besides happy. If what Rich says is true, why didn't Emmy share it with me?

"*Perfect Match* was the only thing Emmy ever asked Armando to do for her," Rich continues when I hand him a glass of water. "And when he said no, she was hurt. When Emmy didn't show up for work on Friday, I worried. Everyone worried. She didn't call or text anyone. We didn't know where she was. Thankfully, we found out she was here. Emmy's never run off like that, Megan. That's when I knew their relationship issues were serious. I worried about my friend and came here to support her. By the time I got here, she and Armando had worked it out. Emmy didn't need my support anymore. I planned to go home today without her ever knowing I was here."

"Rich?" Emmy appears in the doorway between the hall and the living room. "What are you doing here?"

While Emmy and Rich hug and he offers his condolences, I excuse myself and leave the room to give them some privacy.

I wasn't expecting a steady flow of visitors and condolence calls, and our fridge isn't up to the task. After rummaging through the fridge, freezer, and pantry, I find the fixings for a plate of cheese and crackers, two kinds of grapes, and hummus with mini pitas. I plate everything and gather napkins and small plates while the microwave thaws out some cookies from Artsy Tartsy I found in the freezer.

"Look, Emmy, your favourite cookies! Chocolate cherry oatmeal cookies from Artsy Tartsy."

"Not right now, thank you." She forces a small smile. "Maybe later."

"You have to eat something," I say with a sigh.

"You must keep your strength up," Rich reminds her. "Share a cookie with me. You always go on about this wonderful bakery in Harmony Lake. Now I get to see what the fuss is about."

Rich breaks a cookie in half, and puts half on a plate he hands to Emmy, and half on a plate he places on his lap.

"Fine. I'll try," Emmy concedes.

"Thank you," I mouth to Rich from behind Emmy's back.

He smiles and bites into his half of the cookie.

It takes about fifteen minutes for Emmy to finish her half of the cookie, but she does it. She even drinks some apple-spice tea I made for her.

"Poppy!" I jump up when, struggling, Poppy opens the front door. "Let me help you with those."

"Thank you, Megan," she replies, dropping an armful of shopping bags on the floor in the hallway. "The rest is in the car."

I slip on my shoes and go outside to Poppy's open trunk.

"I'm glad I got you alone," Poppy hisses, coming up behind me. "There's been a development."

"What happened?" I drop the bags I'm collecting back in the trunk and spin around to face Poppy.

"Armando's soccer team is issuing a statement

about his death," Poppy replies. "Brad's office sent me a text while I was shopping. They're releasing the statement overnight."

"It will be all over the news when we wake up tomorrow," I say, finishing Poppy's thought.

"And *Hello, today!* is working on a tribute to Armando. They plan to air it tomorrow morning."

"We have to prepare Emmy," I say.

Poppy and I empty the trunk and schlep the rest of the bags into the house.

Poppy and Rich greet each other, neither seeming shocked by the other's presence.

I observe them from a distance as I move the bags out of the hallway. I can understand Rich not being shocked to see Poppy since it makes sense for Emmy's best friend to rush to her side, but why isn't Poppy shocked to see Rich? Did she know he was coming? Or, maybe like me, Poppy suspects Rich is in love with Emmy, and expected him to show up in Harmony Lake.

How can I prepare my grieving sister for the surge of attention when Armando's team releases their press release about his death? And, if Emmy is on bereavement leave, and Rich is in Harmony Lake, who will host the show tomorrow?

Rich announces that he has to leave, and Emmy walks him to the door. They hug, and he says the usual platitudes about being there for her if she needs anything.

"I'll walk you to your car," I offer, holding the door for Rich.

"Thank you for visiting, and for convincing Emmy to eat something."

"It was only half a cookie," Rich reminds me with a chuckle.

"But it's half a cookie more than she would've eaten if you didn't persuade her," I say as he presses the button on the key chain that unlocks the car. "I hear the show plans to air a tribute to Armando tomorrow," I say. "Poppy and I will warn Emmy. In case she asks, who's hosting the show tomorrow? Emmy's on bereavement leave, and you're in Harmony Lake."

"Thanks to the miracle of satellite technology, I'll host on location from Harmony Lake," Rich explains. "Our producer, Sonia Chang came to Harmony Lake with me, and the network dispatched a film crew to join us when they heard about Armando."

This makes the knot in my stomach tighten. It feels predatory that the network's response to Armando's death was to send a film crew to the location.

"You don't expect Emmy to co-host with you, right?" I gasp. "She can't work the day after her husband died."

"Of course not. We'll do an on-air tribute to Armando, but Emmy won't be there. I'll broadcast live from locations close to Harmony Lake. I'll do fewer segments than usual, and the folks at our satellite stations will do more segments than usual. It'll be fine," Rich assures me, like the show is my biggest concern.

I don't give two hoots about the show. Emmy is my biggest concern, followed by the rest of my family, friends, and neighbours.

CHAPTER 13

MONDAY, October 4th

Before leaving the sanctuary of my bedroom, I sit on the bed, cross my legs, and take a few deep breaths. I had hoped a shower and clean clothes would give me a fresh perspective, help make sense of Armando's death, and make my sister's grief less painful to watch. It didn't. The situation is still horrible, and we still don't know how Armando died. The only difference is I'm cleaner and smell better. In hindsight, it was a lot to expect from a fifteen-minute shower and a clean outfit.

"How was your night?" Eric asks, entering the bedroom and closing the door behind him.

"I slept with Emmy," I reply. "I should say, I stayed with Emmy. There wasn't much sleep."

"I figured," Eric replies, kissing my forehead and sitting across from me on the bed. "I got home late, and you weren't in bed, so I assumed you were with Emmy. I heard you get up a few times, but I didn't want to interrupt."

"Where is Emmy?" I ask.

"She fell asleep on the sofa in the family room," Eric replies. "I covered her with a blanket, and Sophie is with her."

"Thank you for looking after her while I showered," I say, rubbing the back of his hand. "Did she eat or drink anything before she fell asleep?"

"I warmed up some of the soup Connie dropped off yesterday. Emmy had a few spoonfuls, and she picked at a fresh orange-cranberry croissant from Artsy Tartsy."

"April was here?" I ask. "She promised she would stay with her family and finish her trip."

"April wasn't here," Eric assures me. "She sent Phillip to the bakery. He dropped off the croissants along with a ton of other pastries and more flowers."

Phillip Wilde is my next-door neighbour at home and work. He owns Wilde Flowers, the florist shop beside Knitorious.

"Good," I say. "I'm glad she didn't rush home."

"Wait until you see how much food we have. Our kitchen has more food than most restaurants. And the flowers! We have more flowers in the house than Phillip has at Wilde Flowers!"

I'm sure Eric is exaggerating about the amount of food and flowers, but between the homemade chicken noodle soup Connie dropped off last night when she brought Sophie home, the pastries from April, and the various casserole dishes and other comfort food from friends and neighbours, our fridge went from almost empty to overflowing. Most of the food arrived last night. Armando's death became public after midnight, but thanks to Harmony Lake's over-achieving rumour mill, our friends and neighbours had a head start.

"There's a list," I remark with no context. "I'll show you how to use it."

"A list?" Eric asks, like he didn't hear me. "You'll show me how to use a list?"

I nod. "For the food. When someone drops off something, we have to add it to the list. Who it's from, what they brought, and what their dish looks like. Also, we have to label their dish. To make sure we thank everyone and return the correct dishes to the correct people."

"OK." Eric says. He leans against the headboard of the bed, and I lean into him, listening to the rhythmic beating of his heart. "How was Hannah when you told her about Armando?"

"She wanted to come home and be with her Auntie Emmy," I reply. "But picking up Hannah is a nine-hour round trip. I can't leave Emmy that long. Adam doesn't want to be that far away if Emmy needs a lawyer, and Hannah's boyfriend can't pick her up until Thursday."

"I'll pick up Hannah tomorrow if the coroner declares Armando's death accidental or natural causes," Eric offers.

He said *if*. Another clue that Eric thinks Armando was murdered.

"You think Armando was murdered, don't you?"

"I don't know," Eric replies. "I just know Armando's death doesn't make sense unless he had an underlying medical condition. And team doctors monitored his health constantly, so it's hard to believe they wouldn't uncover a life-threatening condition before now. I think we should hope for the best and expect the worst."

"When will you hear from the coroner?"

"His preliminary findings should be available this morning," Eric replies. "He did the autopsy yesterday."

"The coroner hates working on weekends," I point out. "How did you convince him to do an autopsy on a Sunday?"

"I reminded him the public interest in this case means every move we make will be scrutinized."

"Thank you." I stretch to give him a kiss, then rest my head on his chest again, letting the steady rhythm of his heart soothe me.

I know Eric doesn't care whether the coroner gets scrutinized for not doing the autopsy right away; he cares about my sister and her need to know how and why her husband died.

"Emmy wants to watch the *Hello, today!* tribute to Armando," Eric says, interrupting my ability to hear the reliable and reassuring thump of his heartbeat. "But I didn't think you'd want to wake her up, so I set the PVR to record it."

"Good idea," I agree. "Poppy said the network will send Emmy a copy of the tribute later today, but if it's on the PVR, she can watch it as often as she wants until they send it."

"How was your conversation with Brad Hendricks?" I ask.

"He's intense," Eric says. "Is he always that uptight,

or is it because of Armando's death? The man is wound tighter than a two-dollar watch."

"I don't know him well enough to have an opinion," I respond. "I've only met him a few times. Emmy doesn't like him though, and it's obvious he doesn't like her. Did he admit he left the cigarette package in Armando's room?"

"Yes, he did." Eric stretches his neck and looks down at me. "How did you figure that out?"

"Lucky guess." I shrug. "Brad smelled like cigarette smoke when I hugged him yesterday. I figured he was in Armando's room, smoked on the balcony, and left the empty package behind."

"Well done, babe. Maybe you should be the investigator."

"And you'll look after Emmy?"

"On second thought, I'll investigate. You comfort your sister." He sighs. "Brad admits the cigarette package was his, and the brand we found in Armando's room matches the brand that Brad had in his pocket when I took him to the station. Forensics will confirm it when they process the package, and the butts we found on the balcony."

"How long will that take?"

"Later today or tomorrow at the latest," Eric replies. "Brad said he was in Armando's room on Saturday morning, before Emmy arrived. He said they had breakfast from room service, then went to the gym together. Brad claimed he hasn't been in Armando's room since. According to Brad, Armando texted him on Saturday afternoon to tell him Emmy was moving into his hotel suite, and they were working out their issues. He says that was the last communication he had with Armando."

"Was Brad disappointed they got back together?"

"He wasn't happy about it."

"He said that?" I ask, incredulous as I push myself off Eric's chest and into a sitting position. "What kind of person hopes his best friend's marriage falls apart?"

"According to Brad, it's not that he *doesn't like* Emmy, it's that she distracted Armando. In Brad's opinion, Armando was a better soccer player before Emmy came along."

"Emmy wanted Armando to fire Brad and sign with a different agent."

"Brad said he's a highly sought-after agent. He has a long waiting list of athletes who want to sign with him. He claims Armando never mentioned firing him or signing with someone else. Brad is very proud of the fact that no client has ever fired him. Ever. He even mentions it in his bio on his company's website."

"Did Brad have a key to Armando's room? Does he have an alibi for yesterday morning?"

"Why would Brad Hendricks have a key to Armando's room?" Eric asks.

"Because he booked the room. The reservation was in Brad's name."

"I'll ask the hotel if they issued Brad a key to both rooms," Eric says, unlocking his phone and tapping on the screen. "As for his alibi, Brad says he was in the gym on the second floor all of Sunday morning. I'm waiting for the hotel to send the access records for Brad's room and the gym to confirm his alibi."

If Emmy is telling the truth, and Armando planned to switch agents for the sake of their marriage, Brad's perfect record would be tarnished. He wouldn't be able to brag about never being fired. His company would have to update his bio on their website. Would Brad Hendricks murder his best friend to save his reputation?

Stop thinking like that, Megan. There's no proof Armando was murdered.

Yet.

CHAPTER 14

"Do you want to watch Armando's *Hello, today!* tribute and montage?" Emmy asks, queuing the PVR.

"Yes," I say.

I join her and Sophie on the sofa, stealing some of the blanket.

Before Emmy presses play, Eric's phone rings, and he glances at the screen.

"I want to watch the montage, but it's the coroner," he says, holding up his phone.

"Take it!" Emmy commands, sweeping him out of the room with a flick of her wrist. "You can watch it later. The coroner is more important."

With a nod, Eric puts the phone to his ear and disappears down the hall.

The wordless montage and tribute to Armando is heartbreaking. He was so young and healthy and full of life. Video clips and still photos fade in and out, accompanied by music.

"Do you recognize the song?" Emmy asks. "It's the first song we ever danced to."

"I remember," I say, dabbing my tears with the edge of the blanket.

Snippets of Armando's life with Emmy, footage of him on the soccer pitch, and Armando's appearances at media and charity events dance across the screen. The song ends with a close-up of Armando and Emmy, arm-in-arm on a red carpet, smiling, then it fades to a photo of Armando in his team uniform, grinning with his arms crossed in front of his chest, resting his foot on a soccer ball. His name and dates of birth and death appear across the bottom of the screen.

We watch the tribute twice. The second time, Emmy pauses each image and video clip to explain where and when it happened.

It's a beautiful tribute, but it seems incomplete. Aside from Armando, Emmy, and his teammates, there are no other people. No family, no friends, and besides soccer photos and footage, nothing before he met Emmy.

"I'll be right back," Emmy says, crying. She throws the blanket off of her legs. "I just need a minute alone."

Before I can offer to leave instead, she's gone, and the door to the guest room closes with a thud.

"Where's Emmy?" Eric asks when he returns from his phone call.

"She'll be right back," I reply. "She needed a minute alone." I lift the blanket and tap the sofa seat. "Do you want to watch the tribute?"

"Later," Eric replies, joining me under the blanket. "How was it?"

"Sad," I respond. "And kind of lonely."

"Lonely?"

I explain to Eric how the montage focused on Armando's professional soccer career and his life with Emmy, but nothing else.

"There were no friends, no baby pictures, and no family photos. It's like Armando didn't exist professionally until he made the major leagues, and he didn't exist personally until he met Emmy. Doesn't that seem strange to you?"

"It's possible the network couldn't include those photos or video clips without permission from the people in them," Eric reasons. "Armando died yesterday, and they had the tribute ready to air early this morning. Maybe they didn't have enough time to get permission."

"You could be right," I concur.

"And Armando was a professional athlete," Eric adds. "Soccer was his biggest focus since he was a little kid. Maybe his only friends were teammates and other soccer people. He spent all his time practicing, working out, and travelling to games."

"And Emmy said Armando didn't communicate with his family, so if they have all his baby pictures and stuff, it would've been difficult to get them. Speaking of Armando's family, did someone notify them?"

"Emmy was Armando's next of kin, and she already knows. I don't have a duty to notify anyone else."

"What about his family in Ecuador?" I ask. "I know

they didn't communicate, but they'd want to know he died, wouldn't they?"

"Brad told Emmy he'd take care of it. I didn't ask him for details. But now that Armando's death is a murder investigation, I'll contact Brad and ask him specifics about Armando's family history."

"What?"

I jolt to an upright position and perfect my posture.

Sophie bounds into the room and jumps on the sofa. The padding of Emmy's bare feet on the hardwood floor grows louder as she gets closer to the family room.

"How did my husband die?" Emmy asks Eric from the doorway to the kitchen.

"PULMONARY ASPIRATION INDUCED ASPHYXIATION," Emmy mutters to herself like she's memorizing a new-to-her foreign phrase.

She stares into the distance, contemplating the tongue-twisting medical term. It's quite a mouthful. I pull the blanket higher, covering us almost to the shoulders. Annoyed that I interrupted her nap, Sophie moves from our laps to the sofa cushion next to me with a sigh.

"Pulmonary means it relates to the lungs, right? My husband had a problem with his lungs?"

"The contents of Armando's stomach went down his windpipe and into his lungs, preventing him from breathing," Eric explains. "Asphyxiation means oxygen deprivation, and aspiration refers to inhaling a foreign substance."

Emmy nods, and a glint of comprehension flashes in her eyes.

"He choked on vomit."

"Yes," Eric confirms.

"Gut rot," I say, flashing back to my conversation with Deb Kee in the hotel lobby.

"I'm sorry?" Eric tilts his ear toward me.

"The reason Armando vomited," I explain, giving Emmy's hand a hopeful squeeze under the blanket. "Deb said the resort was short staffed because of a stomach bug making its way through the employees. They nicknamed it gut rot. Maybe the gut rot jumped from employees to guests, and Armando caught it."

"I'll mention it to the coroner," Eric says, making a note. "But it doesn't fit his findings."

"If Armando choked on vomit, there was something in his stomach," Emmy declares, connecting the dots of her husband's death. "Since room service delivered the food *after* we left, it proves Armando died *after* Megan and I went to brunch. He was alive when I left."

"Makes sense," I concur.

"There was food in Armando's stomach, food from the tray in the room. And you're right, room service delivered the food after you left, but…"

"This means Armando didn't die because I put a nicotine patch on his back while he slept, right?" Emmy asks, interrupting Eric's explanation.

The relief in her voice is palpable, and her eyes swell with fresh tears, but unlike the rest of the tears she's cried since yesterday, these are tears of relief. Relief that her hair-brained nicotine scheme didn't kill her husband.

Eric takes in a deep breath and rubs the back of his neck, then exhales.

"It's unlikely, but it's not that simple," he says.

"Did the nicotine patch make him throw up?" Emmy asks.

"No, a combination of Rohypnol and Fentanyl did."

"What?" Emmy and I demand, in stereo.

"The coroner found both drugs in Armando's system," Eric says, looking at Emmy. "Did Armando use recreational drugs?"

"No! Of course not!"

"I didn't think so, but I had to ask," Eric asserts.

"Do people take Rohypnol recreationally?" I ask, wondering why someone would want to knock Armando unconscious.

"You'd be surprised," Eric says, nodding.

Eric explains that Rohypnol is a date rape drug. It's tasteless and renders the victim unconscious. They often wake up with no memory of what happened while they were under its influence. Fentanyl is a strong opioid painkiller. Even a tiny amount can cause death. A combination sounds like a cocktail for murder. This doesn't strike me as an accidental overdose.

"Armando had regular drug testing," Emmy adds. "His team outsources drug testing to a third party. The tests are blind. The players' names aren't associated with their samples, so no one can alter them. Armando passed every drug test he ever had. And he was vehemently anti-drug. He wouldn't even take aspirin for a headache."

Yet she drugged him with nicotine, anyway. Oh, Emmy.

"If Armando didn't drug himself…"

"Someone else drugged him." I finish Eric's sentence. "But not Emmy!" I add. "The evidence proves he was awake when we left."

"In theory, Armando could have been drugged right before you left," Eric asserts. "He could have answered the door, eaten, then feeling the effects of the drugs, gone back to bed thinking he was ill."

"He could've been drugged right *after* we left too," I chime in. "Same scenario, but with someone other than Emmy as the killer."

"Both options are feasible until we rule out one of them."

"How did the drugs get into his system?" Emmy asks. "Did the coroner find injection marks?"

"We're waiting for forensics to process the food, and for results of some toxicology tests, but the coroner suspects Armando ingested it. Someone contaminated his food or drink." Eric shrugs. "But he hasn't ruled out that someone could have…"

"Laced his nicotine patch?" Emmy deduces.

"We found the discarded patch in the trash can, just like you said. Forensics is testing it to make sure it doesn't contain anything it shouldn't. They're testing the unused patches too. The results should come back today."

"This makes no sense," I plead to Eric. "You always

say follow the evidence, but the evidence doesn't point to Emmy. If she dosed Armando with a lethal combination of drugs, she wouldn't discard the used patch in the room, then tell you. And if the drugs were in the patch, Armando would have been dead or too drugged to answer the door and eat."

"Right now, Emmy, you're the only person we know had access to Armando to drug him, and you have a history of drugging him without his consent."

"And I made that stupid remark to Adam and Megan at brunch," Emmy says, slapping her palm against her forehead and shaking her head. "I'm not saying anything else without my lawyer."

Emmy reaches out of the blanket and unlocks her phone and taps the screen. I presume she's texting Adam.

What remark did she make to Adam and me at brunch? *Think, Megan, think!* So much happened yesterday that everything before we found Armando's body is a blur. What self-incriminating thing did Emmy say?

I'm replaying the events of yesterday morning in my mind when my phone dings, interrupting me just as I mentally relive Emmy and I getting in the car to go to Adam's condo.

"A text from Hannah," I tell Emmy. "She's asking how you are. She didn't text you in case you're sleeping."

"I'll text her in a minute," Emmy responds. "She reminds me so much of you, Sis."

That's it! I remember! Emmy just came back inside

from talking to Poppy on the balcony. We were talking about how divorce affects families, and she said Hannah is resilient like us. Then I commented, I hope none of us gets divorced again, and she said, *I'd rather be a widow than go through another divorce.*

If she didn't bring it up, I wouldn't have remembered. Now that I remember, I have to tell Eric. It would be wrong not to.

Eric's phone rings, and he excuses himself to take the call.

"Why did you mention it in front of Eric?" I hiss, nudging her ribs.

"Mention what?" Emmy hisses back.

"The thing you said at brunch. You incriminated yourself. You should've talked to Adam before you mentioned it to Eric."

"I assumed you or Adam already told him what I said."

"I forgot about it until you mentioned it. And I don't know if Adam remembers either."

"I didn't mean it the way it sounded. I didn't mean I'd kill Armando before I'd divorce him, but considering everything that's happened, it sounds… like…"

Emmy pauses, searching for the right word.

The word she's searching for is motive. It sounds like a motive.

CHAPTER 15

SOPHIE SNIFFS a different spot on the same tree she's been sniffing for three minutes. This is fine with me because I'm in no hurry to get home. We can extend this walk forever, and it would suit me just fine. It's better than watching grief slowly strangle the life out of Emmy and ignoring the unspoken tension between me and Eric because he's investigating my sister for murder.

"Where's Emmy now?" April asks through my Airpods after I tell her about Armando's cause of death and Emmy's position at the top of Eric's suspect list.

"At home," I reply. "Poppy is with her. Eric went to work. Later today, we're going to Adam's office so Eric can ask Emmy more questions. Poppy offered to stay at the house and answer the door while we're gone. I showed her how to update the list when someone drops off food."

"It's a good thing Knitorious is closed on Mondays," April says. "What will you do tomorrow?"

"I'll only work half a day, and Poppy will stay with Emmy."

Ready to move along to the next tree, Sophie trots ahead of me until she reaches the full length of her leash.

"I'm sure Eric knows Emmy didn't kill Armando," April assures me.

"Eric, the future-brother-in-law might know, but Eric the cop needs evidence."

"Did Poppy get the gossip website to delete the post about Emmy and Armando?"

"I don't know," I admit. "I forgot about that stupid post."

"Want me to check if it's still there?" April asks.

"You're already checking, aren't you?"

"Maybe. It depends. Do you *want* me to check?"

"Do it."

"Already done. I opened the website while we argued about it. Do you want the good news or the bad news?"

"Good news," I reply. "I don't think I can handle more bad news."

"They deleted the post."

"Good job, Poppy!" I sigh. "What's the bad news."

"There's a new post about Emmy. Should I read it to you?"

"Yes, please. And can you send me the link?"

The headline is, *Soccer Star's Life Ends in Sudden Death.*

I scoff at the author's flippant use of a soccer pun for such a serious subject.

Sudden death is the term used when the next goal ends the game and determines the outcome. The article below the insensitive headline reads: *Everyone's favourite morning television host is saying, Goodbye, love! after her husband died under mysterious circumstances at an undisclosed location. Our thoughts and prayers are with the grieving widow who lost her perfect match this morning. The soccer widow is grieving in private, at a harmonious lakeside location, under the watchful eye of her sister, a notorious yarn wrangler with a reputation for getting tangled up in murder investigations. According to our sources, the widow's long-suffering co-host raced to her side with impure intentions, hoping after everything is dead and buried, she'll look at him and say Hello, number four!*

"That's horrible!" I shout, picking up speed because I want to get home and erase this cruel, toxic excuse for gossip from the virtual universe. "I want to know who wrote it and who tipped them off."

"All the blog posts on this website have something in common," April observes. "They're about people associated, either directly or indirectly, with the network that airs *Hello, today!* Most of the posts are about the celebrities who appeared on *Perfect Match*."

"Are you suggesting the network, or the people who work on *Perfect Match* run the blog?" I ask. "As a promotional platform for their shows and stars?"

"I don't know," April replies. "But whoever leaked this… this… trash, has inside information. The time-stamp at the bottom of the article is yesterday afternoon."

"They posted it before Armando's death was

announced," I say, putting it all together. "And they referred to me, Knitorious, Harmony Lake, and that I've helped Eric with his previous enquiries. It could be someone local. A friend or neighbour."

"And they hinted Emmy lost her chance to be on *Perfect Match* when Armando died. They even made a dig about Armando being her third husband," April points out.

"They know Rich Kendall is in town and hinted that he has feelings for her. Something I've long suspected."

Who would know all this information? Are multiple people working together? The article says, *according to our sources*. Plural. Maybe they're getting information from multiple people.

"What if the person or people behind these disgusting posts killed Armando?" April asks.

"Then I look forward to exposing them for the murdering scum they are."

ROUNDING THE CORNER TOWARD HOME, Sophie and I walk so fast I almost break into a run. Almost. I can't wait to show Poppy the article and get her to do whatever she does to get it removed. With any luck, she can get the website to delete it before Emmy finds out about it.

"Rich," I wheeze when I spot his car in the driveway.

I stop to catch my breath and pull myself together, so I don't charge into the house like an out-of-shape hysterical person. I open the link April sent and take screenshots of the article, in case whoever posted it deletes it. Then I text the link to Eric, asking if he found out who's behind these posts. He texts me back saying the cyber unit is looking into it. He said something about IP addresses, but I'm not as technically inclined as he gives me credit for.

I compose myself, take one more deep breath, and proceed home.

"Hi, everyone," I say, bending at the knees to detach Sophie's leash.

We exchange greetings, and I join everyone in the living room while Sophie trots to her water bowl in the kitchen.

"Megan, I don't think you've met Sonia Chang," Emmy says, gesturing at the familiar woman in the armchair. "Sonia is our executive producer."

"We haven't met," I say to Sonia. "But I'm a huge fan of your work." I extend my hand, and when Sonia shakes it, I'm a little star-struck.

"It's lovely to meet you, Megan. I'm sorry for your family's loss."

Before becoming the executive producer for *Hello, today!* Sonia Chang was a respected investigative journalist. Her exposés on human rights issues, political scandals, and corporate agendas helped topple governments, CEOs, and other powerful people who used their wealth and influence to exploit the vulnerable masses.

Sonia sits in one armchair, and Poppy sits in the other. Rich sits next to Emmy on the loveseat, and I take a seat on the sofa. Sophie sits at my feet, dripping water from her chin to the floor and still panting from our walk around the neighbourhood.

A tray of pastries and fixings for coffee and tea crowd the coffee table. Someone assumed the role of hostess in my absence.

Emmy, Poppy, Rich, and Sonia are discussing work stuff. I smile and nod politely, pretending to follow along.

Emmy is quiet and distracted. Her face is heavy with exhaustion. She's physically in the same room as us, but mentally she's somewhere else.

Rich doesn't take his eyes off Emmy. He leans in and mutters something close to her ear, causing the corners of her mouth to curl into a brief, weak smile. No matter who is talking, Rich remains fixated on Emmy. Every so often, he gives her knee a reassuring tap or rubs the top of her hand. He loves her; it's so obvious, it's almost tangible.

Poppy is her usual self and attentive to everyone in the room. Is she oblivious to Rich's infatuation with Emmy or ignoring it? I get the sense she's accustomed to it.

Sonia Chang oozes quiet confidence. Her posture is perfect yet relaxed. Her delicate features and perfectly coiffed, conservative chin-length bob contrast with her rabble-rousing reputation. She looks too small and quiet to lead a revolt against the powers-that-be and expose corruption. She shoots the occasional sideways glance at Rich, and I detect a flash of contempt in her expression when she catches him rubbing Emmy's arm. Is the contempt aimed at Rich, Emmy, or both of them?

"Can I get you a drink, Megan?" Poppy asks, interrupting my people watching.

I figured she was the stand-in hostess.

"No, thank you, Poppy. I'll get it. Can I get anyone else a drink?" I smile at the shaking heads and polite smiles. "I'll refresh the tea while I'm in the kitchen." I collect the teapot from the coffee table and disappear into the kitchen.

As I plug in the kettle, a rustling behind me catches my attention.

"Those are beautiful," I comment on the large arrangement of fresh-cut flowers wrapped in kraft paper and tied with black twine.

"They're from Sonia and Rich," Poppy says, sniffing the bouquet.

"Are Sonia and Rich a couple?" I ask, thinking that if they are, Sonia's contemptuous glare at Rich doting on Emmy is justified.

"No," Poppy replies with a giggle. "They definitely are not a couple."

The way she says it makes me think there's more to their story. Rich and Sonia must have a history.

"You said the flowers are from both of them, so I wasn't sure."

"They delivered them on behalf of the *Hello, today!* cast and crew," Poppy clarifies.

"Ahh," I say. "Emmy doesn't mention Sonia often. Did I pick up on some tension between either Sonia and Rich or Sonia and Emmy? Is there anything I should know about?"

"Sonia isn't Emmy's biggest fan," Poppy whispers,

sidling up next to me as I fill the teapot with kettle water. "I think Sonia is jealous of the attention Rich gives Emmy. Rich and Sonia have known each other a long time. Sonia was the target of Rich's attention until Emmy started working at *Hello, today!*."

"I see."

Sophie bounds past us and scratches at the back door. I open the door, then put the lid on the teapot.

"Emmy and I couldn't find a vase…"

I forgot Poppy is still carrying the flowers.

"I'll take care of it, Poppy. Just put them on the table." I gesture to the kitchen table. "Thank you for taking care of everyone. I wouldn't have left you alone if I knew people were coming over."

"Don't worry about it." Poppy dismisses my comment with a flick of her wrist. "Did you have a nice walk?"

"It was nice to get out of the house," I admit. "I don't know how you convinced that website to delete the story about Emmy and Armando, but can you do it again?"

Panic flashes across Poppy's face.

"I forgot to contact them. If they took down the post, it wasn't because of me, but I'm glad it's gone. I'm sorry I forgot to deal with it when I got back to the motel last night."

"Don't worry about it," I assure her. "Yesterday was a nightmare. Are you sure you won't reconsider and stay here instead of the motel?"

"I'm fine at the motel," Poppy insists. "And it's only a short drive to see Emmy." Poppy squints like she just remembered something. "You said you want me to contact the website *again*? Did they post another article?"

I nod. "A horrible post about Armando's death."

"Send me the link."

I unlock my phone and send the link to Poppy.

"Eric is looking into it. With any luck, he'll convince them to take it down before Emmy finds out it exists."

"I hope so," Poppy agrees, nodding. "Does Eric know who's behind it?"

"Not yet. The cyber unit is looking into it. He wants to find the mystery blogger and talk to them about Armando's murder."

"He thinks the murderer is the source of the information?" Her eyes are wide, and her mouth hangs open.

"I don't know."

"Does Eric think he'll find the blogger?" Poppy asks.

"He seems confident," I reply, picking up the teapot. "He said something about tracing the blogger's IP address. And he said they might be able to identify the device the blogger used."

"Device?" Poppy asks. "You mean the type of computer they used?"

"Or phone, or tablet, or whatever." I shrug. "I'll drop off the fresh tea, then deal with the flowers."

"Let me take that," Poppy says, reaching for the teapot.

"Thank you," I say, relinquishing it to her. "I'll pop these flowers in a vase and join you in a few minutes."

CHAPTER 16

THE TALL, rectangular crystal vase is heavier than I remember. It came with a floral arrangement someone sent me when my mum died. I used it again about ten years ago when Adam's law firm sent flowers to the house after his grandmother died. Now, I'm using it to arrange flowers in honour of Armando's death. It's a death vase. It only sees the light of day when someone dies.

"Would you mind if I help with those?" Sonia Chang asks, her warm brown eyes smiling as she points to the bouquet I just laid on the counter next to the kitchen sink.

"You'd be doing me a favour," I reply. "I wasn't blessed with a green thumb or an eye for floral arranging."

"I love flowers," Sonia says, taking over the unwrapping of the bouquet. "My parents owned a florist shop. I've been creating floral arrangements since I was a little girl."

"Be my guest," I say, stepping away from the counter.

As I step back from the counter and Sonia steps forward to take my place, I detect a faint scent of cigarette smoke. Behind her, I lean in and inhale. Does Sonia smoke? My nose says she does. The evidence is subtle but undeniable. I don't know why I'm shocked, but I am. For whatever reason, I just assumed she didn't. I guess everyone has a guilty pleasure; mine is expensive yarn, and Sonia Chang's is smoking.

Sonia shows me the proper way to trim a stem and how to ensure the angle is correct, then delegates stem trimming to me. She'll arrange them in the vase. I trim each stem over the kitchen sink and pass the flower to Sonia, who nestles it in the vase.

"I'm a huge fan of your investigative journalism work," I say, trying not to sound like a journalism groupie. "Do you mind if I ask why you left investigative journalism to produce a television morning show?" Sonia sighs, and I fear I've crossed a line. "I understand if it's none of my business. Please don't feel obliged to tell me."

I pass her a white lily and pick up a sprig of Italian ruscus.

"Love," Sonia replies with breathless nostalgia. "When the network offered Rich the co-host position at *Hello, today!* he broke up with me. He said our schedules were incompatible. Rich had a fixed, Monday-to-Friday schedule, and I flew around the world on assignment. Sometimes for weeks at a time."

"I didn't know you and Rich were together." I hand her a stem of bells of Ireland.

"*Were*," she echoes. "We *were* together. I took the producer job so we could stay together. Rich promised me a life of domestic bliss. He promised me kids, dogs, and a cozy suburban life, so I took the producer job and pivoted *my* life to accommodate *his* career."

"What happened?" I ask, cutting another lily.

"He fell in love with Emmy and dumped me."

"I'm sorry, Sonia," I say, handing her the lily. "When did this happen?"

"When the network hired your sister to fill the co-host position on *Hello, today!*" she replies, stabbing the lily into the centre of the arrangement. "I auditioned for the co-host job, but I didn't get it."

She jabs another sprig of Irish bells into the vase, her floral arranging becoming increasingly aggressive the more she talks about her relationship with Rich and the sacrifices she made for him.

"Wow," I say, stunned that the network wouldn't want a journalist of Sonia's calibre to host their flagship morning show.

"They said viewers would always associate me with the intense, investigative reports they knew me for," Sonia continues. "They said viewers wouldn't accept me as a fun, bubbly, morning show host. Emmy got the co-host spot, and I got to keep my job as executive producer." She stabs a white rose into the arrangement. "If I'd gotten the job, Miranda Monroe would never have entered our lives, and Rich and I would still be together," she says, using Emmy's professional name and fussing combatively with the flowers in the vase. "We'd probably be at home right now in our cozy suburban house, playing with our golden retriever and making lunch for our kids." She flashes me a strained smile.

Could Sonia Chang hate my sister enough to kill Armando? There's no doubt Sonia is smart enough to frame Emmy for the crime, and she arrived in Harmony Lake before Armando died. Maybe Sonia killed Armando to make Emmy as miserable as Sonia was when Rich left her. Maybe Sonia wanted to give Emmy a taste of her own medicine. Or maybe she hoped the network would fire Emmy because of the negative publicity, thereby eliminating her from the show and from Rich's life.

"Listen, Megan, your sister should get a lawyer," Sonia says in a gentle voice, like she's telling me bad news and is sad she's the messenger.

I'm tempted to tell her Emmy already has a lawyer, but I don't.

"Why would you say that?" I ask.

"Because I think it's possible Emmy found out something about Armando. Something big. Something that made her angry enough to kill him."

I open my mouth to ask Sonia what she's talking about when Emmy and Rich come into the kitchen.

"Such beautiful flowers," Emmy says, admiring the flowers in the vase. "Can I help arrange them?"

"Sonia and I will take care of it," I insist, trimming another white rose.

"Let us do this for you," Sonia adds, sounding

almost friendly toward Emmy.

"I thought it would be good for Emmy to get some fresh air," Rich says, guiding Emmy toward the back door with his hand on the small of her back.

"Good idea," I agree. "Sophie's already out there waiting for you."

"When Poppy gets off the phone, can you tell her we're on the back deck?" Emmy asks.

"Will do."

With Rich and Emmy outside, I check the living room for Poppy. I'd rather not have any eavesdroppers overhear my conversation with Sonia. I spot Poppy through the living room window. She's standing on the driveway, squinting into the sun, with her phone to her ear.

"What did you mean when you said Emmy found out something about Armando?" I ask Sonia while trimming another stalk of Irish bells, thankful there are only a few untrimmed stems left. "They argued about a reality TV show," I hiss, handing her the trimmed foliage.

"I know," Sonia acknowledges. "The producer of *Perfect Match* is a close friend of mine. I'm the person who suggested to him that Emmy and Armando would be good contestants. And I know Brad spun a yarn about reality TV reducing the value of Armando's brand, but there's another reason Armando didn't want to take part in the show." She stops fussing with the blooms and looks me in the eye. "Emmy wasn't Armando's first wife. He was married to someone else before he married your sister."

"OK." I shrug, relieved Sonia didn't drop a huge bombshell of controversy on me. "So was Emmy. Even if Armando didn't tell her about his first marriage, she'd get over it." I shrug again. "At our age, everyone has a past. Emmy was married twice before she married Armando."

"Your sister's prior marriages ended in divorce," Sonia explains. "Armando's didn't."

I gasp and bring my hand to my mouth.

"Oh my! Armando's first wife died? He was a widower?"

Sonia shakes her head.

"The first Mrs. Garcia is alive and well in Baña, Ecuador. They never divorced."

"Annulment?" I suggest, hoping Sonia will nod in agreement.

"No annulment, no divorce, no death. In the eyes of the law, Armando was married to his first wife when he died."

If this is true, Emmy isn't Armando's widow. His real widow is in Ecuador.

"You're mistaken," I insist, shaking my head and dropping the shears in the sink.

"I'm not." Sonia's voice and demeanor exude an abundance of confidence and a hint of smugness. "I wish I was."

Hmph. Somehow, I doubt that.

"Why were you investigating Armando in the first place?"

"Someone contacted me with an anonymous tip. The tip was about something else, but when I started looking into it, my investigation led me to Armando's first wife."

"What was the tip about?"

"Corruption in major league sports." Sonia waves her hand and shakes her head as if it doesn't matter. "Major league sports is full of corruption, but it's hard to prove. The power and money are concentrated in such a small number of stakeholders," she explains, getting off track. "Anyway, I couldn't prove the tipster's allegation."

"What was the allegation?"

"It's irrelevant, Megan. Nothing came of it. What I just told you about Armando's real wife is what's important."

"Do you have proof?"

"I was an investigative reporter, remember? I know how to confirm a story and double-check the facts."

I disappear from the kitchen and reappear seconds later, holding out Adam's business card.

"Can you send the proof to this lawyer?" I ask.

"Sure," Sonia replies, taking the card and reading it. "But I also have to send it to the police. I'm sure being the future wife of a police chief, you understand." Sonia smiles and her eyes glisten with the same contempt as when she watched Rich comfort Emmy in the living room.

"Totally," I say, handing her Eric's card with my other hand. "Here's the police chief's contact information." I smile. "Thanks for filling me in, Sonia."

And giving the police another motive for Emmy to kill her husband.

CHAPTER 17

ME: Sonia Chang is sending you alleged proof that Armando was a bigamist.

Adam: Does Emmy know about this?

Me: No.

Adam: Don't tell her until I verify it.

I reply with a thumbs-up emoji.

"Where is everyone?" Poppy asks.

Distracted by Armando's potential bigamy, I didn't hear her come in.

"Back deck," I say, then look up from my phone. "Is everything OK? You were out there for a while."

"Everything is fine." Poppy smiles. "Yesterday when I picked up Emmy's essential items, I couldn't find a specific product Emmy uses daily. I substituted with another brand, and Emmy got upset. She went on about her life being hard enough without worrying about her skin reacting to a different moisturizer. She lectured me about her very sensitive skin and how it breaks out if she changes her skin care routine. And when she eventually faces the world, all eyes will be on her, and she doesn't want the headlines to focus on her skin. You know how she is."

"Oh," I say awkwardly. "I'm sorry, Poppy. Emmy isn't herself right now. She's in shock and…"

Poppy raises her hand like a girl scout to stop me from talking.

"I understand, Megan. But Emmy would react like that even if her husband didn't die. It is what it is." She shrugs. "You don't see it. You live far away and don't interact with her every day."

"Umm…" I'm not sure how to respond to Poppy's rant, but I feel like I should defend Emmy, especially since she's in no state to defend herself right now.

"Anyway," Poppy continues, "I called the manufacturer to ask where the closest seller is in this neck of the woods, and they just called me back."

"Oh. I'll get it. Tell me what and where it is."

"No need. When they heard who it was for, they offered to send Emmy free samples by overnight courier. One of the many perks of Miranda Monroe's charmed life." Poppy shrugs. "Her nighttime moisturizer should arrive on your doorstep sometime tomorrow."

Charmed life? Has Poppy forgotten that my sister, her best friend, was widowed yesterday?

I guess Armando's death is taking a toll on everyone, not just Emmy. It seems Poppy is straining under the pressure of all the demands that come with being Emmy's PA and best friend. I've never heard Poppy say anything critical about Emmy before. Since it's a one-off, I'll attribute her rant to stress and let it go.

I turn my attention back to my phone.

Me: Can we talk?

Eric: Of course. Work or personal?

How do I answer that? In this case, his work is my personal.

Me: Yes.

Eric: Do you want me to call you?

Me: In person?

Eric: Where?

When I arrive at Knitorious, Eric is already there, sitting on the sofa in the cozy sitting area. There's a to-go cup from Latte Da on the coffee table. I know without asking it's a chocolate caramel latte for me.

"It's not like you to drink coffee past noon," I say, joining him on the sofa and kissing him hello.

"It's for you," he says. "But I think you already knew that."

"I had a hunch," I admit. "The super-hot, local police chief likes to surprise me with coffee."

"It's probably just his excuse to see you during the day."

"He doesn't need an excuse," I say, then give him another kiss before I crack the lid on my chocolate caramel latte and take the first glorious sip. "Thank you for meeting me here. It's the only place I could think of where no one would interrupt us."

"How's your day?" he asks, massaging the back of my neck.

"Longer than a marathon," I reply, leaning into his touch. "Yours?"

"Busier than a moth in a yarn store," Eric replies with a muffled chuckle.

"Not funny," I say, laughing and gesturing to yarn store we're sitting in.

"How's Emmy?"

"Tired. Rich and Sonia came over to visit her. Then she went for a nap. Poppy is staying with her until I get home."

"Listen babe, I've been thinking," Eric says. I pivot my hips so I'm facing him. He moves his hand from my neck to my knee. "Maybe someone else should investigate Armando's murder."

"Who? You're the only murder investigator the HLPD has."

"I can borrow someone from another town. You were right yesterday. Maybe I can't be both a cop and a fiancé. Being there for you and our family takes priority over investigating a murder."

Taken aback by his proposition, I'm not sure what to say.

"Who would investigate it?"

"I'm not sure." Eric shrugs. "I'd find the best investigator around. Someone thorough with an excellent reputation."

"*You're* the best investigator around," I remind him. "*You're* thorough and have an excellent reputation. Do you want to recuse yourself?"

"I want to do what's best for us. I don't want to blur the line between work and home, and I don't want my job to interfere with our relationship."

"If our relationship wasn't a factor, if this investigation didn't cause tension between us, would you want to recuse yourself?"

"No," Eric admits.

"Do you think Emmy killed Armando?"

"No. But right now she's our number one suspect and investigating Armando's murder means investigating your sister."

"I trust you," I say. "I don't know if I'd trust another investigator. You'll follow every lead, and you're open-minded about all the possibilities. I know you'll do whatever it takes to uncover the truth. You won't just charge my sister with murder because you can force the evidence to fit."

"You don't want me to step back, do you?"

"Only if it's what you want."

"How about this? We'll take it day by day. If the line between work and home gets too blurry, or the investigation causes stress in our relationship, I'll step back."

Eric's phone dings and vibrates in his pocket, but he ignores it. I recognize the sound; it's an email notification.

I nod and say, "Good compromise."

He kisses my forehead.

"Now, can I talk to you as a cop for a minute, Chief Sloane?"

Eric sighs. "What's up?"

"There's something I didn't tell you yesterday. I

147

didn't mean to leave it out. I forgot about it until Emmy jogged my memory this morning."

"The brunch conversation Emmy alluded to earlier?"

I nod and take a deep breath. "She didn't mean it. I don't know how she meant it, but she didn't mean it the way it sounded," I say, laying the groundwork for my sister's incriminating statement. "It's not even evidence. It's probably irrelevant, but not telling you feels like lying."

"Just tell me already." He smiles and takes my hand.

I relive the conversation at brunch yesterday and include Emmy's comment about preferring to be a widow over a three-time divorcée.

"If she had just killed her husband with a lethal overdose of drugs, she wouldn't have risked saying it. Emmy's impulsive, not stupid."

"Thank you for telling me," Eric says, without acknowledging whether the self-incriminating statement will impact the evidence against Emmy. His phone buzzes again, and he ignores it again. "I got an email from Sonia Chang a little while ago."

"I know," I say, nodding. "She sent the same information to Adam. Do you think it's true?"

"I'm not sure," Eric replies. "I assigned an officer to verify it. For Emmy's sake, I hope it's not true."

"Because it gives her a motive to kill Armando?"

"Because it will break her heart," he replies.

"Yup," I agree. "Sonia hates Emmy. She has her own reasons to kill Armando."

"I'm listening."

Eric sits upright and produces his small notebook and pen.

"Sonia and Rich were a couple. He dumped Sonia because he fell in love with Emmy."

"Wouldn't that give her a motive to kill Emmy, not Armando?"

"Killing Armando makes Emmy suffer. An eye for an eye. Sonia lost Rich, and Emmy lost Armando."

Eric nods. "I'll look into it."

"Sonia said she discovered Armando's first wife by accident, while she was investigating an unrelated tip. If the unrelated tip led her to Armando, he might have another secret Emmy doesn't know about."

"Did Sonia tell you what the unrelated tip was about?"

"Something about corruption in sports. She wouldn't talk about it, just said she couldn't prove it, and it was irrelevant. Also, I think Sonia might be a smoker."

"Did you observe her smoking?"

"No, but she was beside me at the kitchen sink for several minutes, and she smelled of cigarette smoke. It was faint, but it was nicotine."

"I'll question Sonia." He unlocks his phone, types a quick message, then returns the phone to his pocket. "I'm still waiting for the forensics results on the cigarette package and butts we found. If they don't match Brad, we'll run them against Sonia."

"This gives Rich a motive too," I point out. "If he believed Armando was the only obstacle between him and a happy ever after with Emmy, maybe he removed the obstacle. He was in town before Armando died, and he's already visited Emmy twice since yesterday. It's like he's inserting himself into her life and trying to be her primary support person while she grieves. There's something territorial about it, like when Sophie pees on every tree we walk past."

Eric's phone dings and buzzes again. More email notifications. Are they forensic reports for Armando's case? Part of me wants him to check, and part of me doesn't want to know. I try to put Eric's inbox out of my mind.

"Did you figure out who published the nasty blog posts about Emmy and Armando?" I ask.

"No, but it's not someone local."

"How do you know they aren't local if you don't know who did it?"

"The first post, the one about Armando following Emmy to Harmony Lake, originated from a coffee shop a few blocks from Emmy and Armando's house. The second post, the one about Armando's death, originated from Latte Da."

"That's only a few stores away from Knitorious," I say, shocked. "The mystery blogger followed Emmy to Harmony Lake?"

"That's my conclusion. It can't be Armando, because the second post appeared after he died, but it could be Rich, Sonia, Poppy, or any of the crew who arrived in town yesterday. Has Emmy been to Latte Da?"

"No!" I snap, offended by the suggestion that my sister would reveal intimate details of her life in such a disrespectful manner. "Except for when I walked

Sophie earlier, and now, Emmy and I have been together every minute since we found Armando's body. We haven't been near Latte Da!"

"I'm sorry, babe. I have to ask."

"What about Brad?" I ask, ignoring Eric's apology and keen to change the subject.

"He's still a person of interest. We haven't ruled him out."

"Brad had a lot to lose if Armando fired him," I say. "It would be a blow to his reputation and his ego. He was Armando's confidant. He could be the mystery blogger and Armando's killer."

"I know," Eric replies. "We're investigating all the suspects, not just Emmy."

"There must be a way to determine who followed Emmy to Harmony Lake and visited Latte Da when the mystery blogger posted the article."

"We interviewed the employees who worked at Latte Da yesterday. We showed them photos of the *Hello, today!* cast and crew. They didn't recognize anyone. Well, they recognized Emmy and Rich from seeing them on TV, but they didn't recognize anyone from the coffee shop. They assured us they'll keep their eyes peeled and notify us if any of them visit Latte Da. They'll note the date and time."

"Speaking of employees," I say, "have you inter-viewed the hotel employees who were working when Armando died?"

"Most," Eric replies. "The guy who delivered Armando's breakfast caught that gut rot bug and called in sick today. I hope to interview him tomorrow."

"I should get back to Emmy," I say, standing up.

"And I should get back to the office," Eric responds, also standing up. "I need to go through my inbox before I interview Emmy."

A knot forms in my stomach when I wonder if the forensics reports in Eric's inbox eliminate or further implicate Emmy as Armando's murderer.

CHAPTER 18

"Do you know Rich Kendall is in love with you?" I ask Emmy on the short drive to Adam's law office.

"He told me a long time ago," Emmy replies with no hint of surprise. "I've made it clear to him I don't feel the same way."

With Armando out of the picture, maybe Rich hopes Emmy will reconsider her feelings for him.

"You never mentioned it to me."

"Why would I?" Emmy shrugs. "It's irrelevant. Did Rich tell you he's in love with me?"

"No, I could tell by the way he looks at you," I reply, not revealing that Sonia later confirmed my hunch. "Did anything ever happen between you and Rich?"

"Gawd no!" Emmy chuckles for the first time since Armando died. "I love Armando. I would never cheat on my husband. Besides, it would be unprofessional to have a relationship with someone I work with."

I shift the car into park and turn off the engine.

"We're early," I say. "Shall we sit here for a few minutes?"

"Uh-uh." Emmy shakes her head and looks with determination at the renovated, large Victorian house. "I want to get this over with. I have nothing to hide. I didn't kill my husband, but maybe I have information that will help Eric figure out who did."

"We'll find Armando's killer," I assure her. "The murdering scumbag who did this won't get away with it. I won't rest until they're behind bars."

"Not much," Emmy replies when Eric asks her what she knows about Armando's family. "Armando stopped communicating with his family before I met him. I think his parents live in Ecuador. He said his mum was from Brazil or Belize or something. He had an older... sister? I think?" Emmy says, unsure whether Armando had a sister or whether she was older than him. "I think she emigrated. Armando never talked about his family, and if I asked him about them, he'd change the subject," she says, justifying her lack of information about the family she married into. "He had a best friend who was like a brother, but I don't know his name. They stopped talking because his friend didn't make the major leagues and was jealous when Armando did. His friend had a career-ending knee injury." Emmy huffs, exasperated. "You should ask Brad," she says, clearly frustrated by how little she knows about her husband's past.

"Brad knew Armando longer than me, and I think he knows more about his family."

"Do you know why Armando stopped communicating with his family?" Eric asks.

"Money," Emmy replies. "Armando said they were unhappy with how much money he gave them. He refused to increase the amount he sent them, and they cut him off completely."

"When did they cut him off completely?" Eric asks.

Emmy shrugs and shakes her head. "Sometime before we met."

Could one of Armando's estranged family members have orchestrated his murder? Maybe when Armando stopped sending money, they decided he was expendable. Or maybe they hoped they'd inherit his money.

"Did you hang the DO NOT DISTURB sign on the hotel room door?" Eric asks.

"No," Emmy says, shaking her head. "Someone hung it up after Megan and I left for brunch. I made a mental note to ask Armando about it when I removed it. But I forgot because I found my husband's dead body."

"We only found one DO NOT DISTURB sign in the hotel suite," Eric says, "so it's probable the sign you removed from the door handle was the sign from inside the room. We found your fingerprints on it."

"Because I removed it from the door handle," Emmy reminds him, irritated. "I told you that."

"But your fingerprints were the only ones on the sign."

"Whoever hung it up either wiped off their finger-prints, or wore gloves." Emmy shrugs.

"Can you think of anyone who would want to hurt Armando?" Eric asks.

"A crazed fan or someone who was jealous of him, maybe," Emmy theorizes. "Armando was amazing. He was the complete package. He donated his time and money to underprivileged kids. He visited children's hospitals. He was smart, funny, gorgeous, talented…" Emmy's words fade, and her eyes swell with tears.

"Can you think of anyone specific who might have killed Armando?" Eric clarifies.

Emmy nods.

"After our argument about *Perfect Match*, Armando agreed to fire Brad and find a new agent. One who's more open-minded and doesn't hate me. If Armando told him, Brad could have freaked out and killed him. Brad's ego would never accept being fired or Armando choosing me over him. Brad and Armando are close friends, but I'm not sure how close they'd be if Armando wasn't Brad's client."

"I need a list of everyone who entered the hotel room."

Eric hovers his pen above the paper, ready for names.

"No one. Not while I was there," Emmy replies to Eric's question. "I mean, room service delivered food, but otherwise it was just me and Armando."

"I have the access records for Armando's room," Eric says, flipping through the binder that lays open across his lap. "The door was unlocked six times between when Armando checked in, and when you found him."

"Do you know who unlocked the door six times?" I ask.

Eric opens the binder rings and removes a sheet of paper.

"Armando entered the room after checking in on Friday," Eric read. "Armando entered the room again after visiting the gym that evening. On Saturday, housekeeping entered the room while Armando and Brad were at the gym. Armando returned from the gym. Armando returned later the same day from the pool. Yesterday, Emmy returned to the room after brunch with Megan."

"Hold up," Emmy straightens her spine. "Did you say housekeeping entered the room?"

Eric nods. "Housekeeping entered the room Saturday morning while Armando and Brad were at the gym."

"That's not possible," Emmy says. "Armando declined housekeeping. He always declined housekeeping when he checked into a hotel." She turns to me. "He usually only stayed in one town for a night or two, and he'd rather not have anyone in the room, so he specifically declined housekeeping services."

"Maybe Armando forgot to decline housekeeping this time? Or he requested something and housekeeping brought it to the room?" I suggest. "Like extra towels or pillows, or something."

"That's the only possible explanation," Emmy concedes.

"I'll ask Deb Kee if there's a record of Armando declining housekeeping services or contacting the front desk to get something delivered to his room," Eric says, making a note on the page he just read from.

"Also, Armando eats six times per day. Shouldn't there be a record of room service delivering his food?" Emmy asks. "Someone opened the door to bring the food inside."

"There's only a digital record if a keycard unlocked the door," Eric explains.

"When someone enters the room from the outside," Adam clarifies.

"Right," Eric says. "If Armando opened the door from inside, there wouldn't be a record. Room service employees do not have keycards. Armando had to let them in. He opened the door from inside when room service delivered his food. This is also why there's no digital record of Brad entering the room, Emmy entering the room when she arrived on Saturday, or Megan entering the room when she picked you up for brunch yesterday."

"Because Armando let Brad and I in, and I let Megan in," Emmy concludes. Then she looks at me. "Do you know what this means?"

The killer was someone Armando knew and trusted. He let them in.

CHAPTER 19

TUESDAY, October 5th

The world is wet and grey. The cloudy skies are so dark, the streetlights on Water Street keep flickering on and off even though it's daytime.

"If Armando never divorced his first wife, it explains why he pressured Emmy to elope and skip a big wedding," April says into my Airpods. "He didn't want the attention a big wedding would attract."

"And it explains why he tried to convince Emmy to keep their marriage a secret," I add. "I don't want it to be true, but my instincts tell me it is," I admit.

"Sonia is an experienced investigative journalist," April adds. "She wouldn't tell you unless she had proof to back it up."

"Did I tell you our theory that the mystery blogger is someone who followed Emmy to Harmony Lake?"

"No!" April retorts. "Who is it?"

I tell April that Eric doesn't know who the mystery

blogger is, but he knows where they posted their vile content from.

"I have a hunch it might be Brad," I admit.

"Why?"

"Because he was Armando's confidant, and he knows all the information the blogger alluded to in the posts. Also, the posts were more critical of Emmy than Armando, and Brad is open about his dislike for her."

"Interesting," April says. "I went to the website, and the second blog post was gone. Someone deleted it."

"Good," I scoff.

"Why would they delete the posts about Emmy and Armando, but leave the other posts up?"

"Who knows?" I reply. "Maybe they had an attack of conscience."

While I sweep the floor and replenish a few barren shelves, April updates me on her visit with her family and her cousin's wedding celebration. Like all family events, her cousin's wedding isn't without its share of family drama. But I can't help but feel a twinge of jealousy because April's family drama revolves around the bride's ex-boyfriend attending the nuptials as her best friend's plus one. I'd rather deal with a nuisance ex than a murder investigation any day.

"I think the only thing Emmy ate yesterday was an orange-cranberry croissant from Artsy Tartsy. She's eaten very little since Armando died. I'm afraid if her appetite doesn't improve, she'll get sick," I say after thanking April for sending boxes of fresh pastries to the house yesterday.

The store doesn't open for another ten minutes, but Tina knocks on the window to get my attention.

"Hi!" I shout and wave, even though she can't hear me from the sidewalk.

"Hi?" April asks confused. "Is someone there?"

"Tina," I reply. "It's raining again. I should let her in."

It's been raining off and on all morning. Ten-to-fifteen-minute increments of hard rain, then nothing. Mother nature can't make up her mind.

April and I end our call. I unlock the door and flip the sign from CLOSED to OPEN.

"Hi, Megan," Tina says, taking off her raincoat and laying it on the counter. "How's Emmy doing?"

"Under the circumstances, she's doing as well as you'd expect," I reply.

"Please give her my condolences," Tina says. "Her husband's death shocked everyone at Rise & Glide."

"I forgot you work there," I say. "Did you work on Sunday?"

"I was supposed to," Tina replies, "but I caught that stomach bug that's going around."

"Gut rot," I say with a knowing nod. "How are you feeling?"

"It's a fast and furious bug," Tina informs me. "You feel like you're going to die for twenty-four hours, then it stops." She shrugs, then panic flashes across her face, and she covers her mouth with her hand. "I'm sorry! I shouldn't have said that. About feeling like dying."

"It's fine," I chuckle, waving away her comment. "I know what you meant."

"I finished two Knitted Knockers since I was here on Friday." Tina reaches into her backpack, pulls out a plastic bag and hands it to me. "I dropped a stitch on one of them," she cautions. "I tried to fix it like Connie showed me, but it looks a bit wonky."

"I'm sure it's fine," I assure her. "Connie or I will look at it. If we can fix it, we will." I stash the bag under the counter. "Thank you for using your knitting super-power for good. Sadly, the demand for Knitted Knockers exceeds the supply."

"I could've made a third one except I ran out of yarn," Tina says.

I gesture to the yarn display Connie and I set up for Breast Cancer Awareness Month.

"Everything on these shelves is buy-one-get-one-free until the end of the month."

"I bet Emmy is excited to get back to work," Tina comments as she digs through skeins of yarn.

"She hasn't mentioned work yet. I'm sure she'll go back when she's ready."

"Oh," Tina says, her face clouded with confusion. "Her glam squad is checking in later today. And I over-heard someone say Emmy is working tomorrow."

What happened to the confidentiality agreement hotel employees sign? The one that says they could lose their jobs if they discuss guests outside of work?

"Who said that?" I ask, hoping it's just speculation.

"The Sonia woman talked about it in the dining room last night. She said Emmy's glam squad is due in Harmony Lake today. Two people. Hair and make-up. I checked, and the network made two reservations for today."

"What else did Sonia say?"

"She said the ratings for yesterday's show and the tribute to Emmy's husband were through the roof, and she wants to capitalize on it by doing a segment with Emmy."

Speechless, my mouth is agape. The more I learn about Sonia, the more I dislike her. I'm a fan of her work as an investigative journalist, but I'm not a fan of her as a person.

"I'm sorry," Tina says. "I assumed you knew."

"Sonia talked to you about the show's ratings and Emmy's glam squad?"

"No," Tina chuckles. "She was talking to her dinner companion."

"Who did she have dinner with?"

"Rich Kendall."

"Would you like me to wind these for you?" I ask, ringing up four skeins of yarn for Tina. Tina checks her watch and considers my offer. "You can wait, or you can leave them and come back later."

"It's fine," Tina says with a smile. "I like winding yarn, and I have to skedaddle, or I'll be late for work."

"Connie will be here any minute. She'll be sorry she missed you." I bag Tina's yarn and thank her again for her Knitted Knocker donation. "And thank you for telling me about Emmy's glam squad and her potential return to *Hello, today!*" I say, handing Tina the bag.

"I'm not supposed to talk about guests," Tina

admits. "I'd appreciate it if you didn't tell anyone it was me who told you."

"I'll never reveal my source," I promise.

"I love Harmony Lake. I'm glad I took the job at Rise & Glide and moved here. You and Connie have made me feel welcome. I like Emmy and feel bad for what she's going through, so if I overhear anything else, I'll break the rules and tell you."

"I appreciate it, Tina, but you shouldn't risk getting in trouble or losing your job."

"I want to help," Tina insists. "I've heard about your sleuthing history. You and Chief Sloane have a perfect record for solving crimes. I want to help keep your record perfect."

"That's sweet, but you shouldn't put yourself or your job on the line…"

The bell over the door brings an abrupt end to our conversation.

"It finally stopped raining!" Phillip announces from behind a large floral arrangement of fall-coloured asters, chrysanthemums, and marigolds.

Who are they from? Where will I put them? Our house is full of condolence flowers and food. We're out of empty surfaces.

Tina rushes over to hold the door for him, and he places the vase on the coffee table in the cozy sitting area.

"Gotta go," Tina quips with a wave as the door closes behind her.

"They're gorgeous," I tell Phillip. "Who are they from?"

There's no visible card in the arrangement.

"They're from your future groom," Phillip replies, fussing with the flowers and reorganizing a few blooms. "It's your October bouquet."

Our very first date was to a local fundraiser that included a silent auction. One of the silent auction items was a year's supply of monthly floral arrangements from Wilde Flowers. Eric had the winning bid. When the first year of floral arrangements expired, Eric renewed it for a second year as an anniversary gift. We're nearing the end of my second year of flower deliveries.

"Thank you," I say. "How did you find time to create this masterpiece? You've been so busy with condolence flowers."

"I'm a professional florist, sweetie! We're super-heroes without capes." We laugh. "I delivered them here because I figured you might be out of space at home."

"You figured right," I confirm.

"And I thought you could use something pretty to cheer you up since your brother-in-law died."

"Thank you, Phillip."

While Phillip and I hug, it occurs to me that this is the first time I've seen him since Saturday. Because we're next-door neighbours, I take for granted that we see each other almost every day.

"How's Emmy?" Phillip asks.

"As well as you'd expect under the circumstances," I reply with my standard response.

"How's Eric feeling?" Phillip asks in a hushed tone.

The concerned tone in his voice worries me. He's asking like there's something wrong with Eric that he's not supposed to know about.

"Fine?" I reply, confused.

"Witch hazel," Phillip whispers with a wink. "Trust me. It worked wonders for my mother."

I'm about to ask why he thinks Eric needs witch hazel and what Phillip's mother used it for when the bell over the door jingles and Connie strides into the store.

"Hello, my dear." She hugs me tight and plants a kiss on my cheek. "Hello, Phillip." They give each other a side hug and exchange air kisses. "Where's Sophie?" Connie asks, marveling at the corgi-free space around her ankles, where Sophie usually waits in eager antici-pation for Connie to greet her.

"At home with Emmy and Poppy," I reply. "Emmy likes to have her around."

Connie admires my October floral arrangement and compliments Phillip on his creative mastery, then takes off her jacket.

"I'll be right back," Connie says as she heads toward the back room to hang up her coat. "Oh my!" she declares, stopping at the counter. "Tina was here, wasn't she?" She holds up the jacket that Tina left draped across the counter. "I'll hang it in the back. She must go through so many jackets at the rate she leaves them behind," Connie chuckles on her way to the back room.

"I'll text Tina and let her know she left it here," I call after her.

"I should get back to the shop," Phillip says with a

sigh. "I have to fill an order and deliver it to the most unworthy recipient ever!"

"Who?" I ask, wondering who Phillip has deemed unworthy of his floral artistry.

"I can't even!"

He rolls his eyes and waves his hand in front of his face with a dramatic flourish.

"Yes, you can," I encourage.

"Fine. It's that horrible Sonia woman your sister works with."

Who ordered flowers for Sonia Chang? And what did she do to make Phillip deem her unworthy?

CHAPTER 20

"Who ordered flowers for Sonia?"

"Sonia Chang?" Connie asks, returning from the back room.

I nod and update her on what she missed while she was hanging up jackets.

"It's a corporate order from the Hendricks Agency," Phillip replies.

The Hendricks Agency is Brad's agency. Why would Brad buy Sonia flowers?

"Did they give you a message to write on the card?" I ask.

"Yes." He arches one eyebrow.

"What's the message?"

"Do you regret it yet? B."

Regret what? How vague and cryptic.

"That's it? That's the entire message?" I ask.

Phillip nods.

"I don't care if she won a Pulitzer Prize for Investigative Reporting, Sonia Chang is not a nice person,"

Phillip declares, crossing his arms in front of his chest.

"You've met her?" Connie asks.

"Yesterday," Phillip replies with a huff. "She came into Wilde Flowers with Rich Kendall to get flowers for Emmy."

"The flowers were beautiful, by the way," I interject. "The white and cream blooms with dark green foliage were…" I pinch my thumb and forefinger together and make a chef's kiss. "And I loved the presentation in kraft paper with black twine. Very trendy."

"Do NOT give me credit for that floral arrangement!" Phillip says, giving his foot a dramatic little stomp. "I didn't make it!"

"Who made it?" Connie asks. "Noah?"

Noah is Phillip's apprentice.

"No!" Phillip replies. "Sonia made it."

"You offer self-serve floral arrangements?" I ask, unaware Phillip offered this option.

"No!" Phillip shakes his head. "But that didn't stop Sonia Chang. She said she knew what she wanted. She walked around my shop and went INSIDE my floral cooler." He crosses his arms in front of him. "No one goes inside my floral cooler. She helped herself to whatever she wanted and acted like she owned the place. While she was collecting and arranging MY flowers, SHE gave ME tips for creating bouquets and took it upon herself to FIX arrangements I'd already made."

"Oh my," Connie says, gripping her pearls and shaking her head.

I'm not sure if the "Oh my" is in response to Sonia's

169

behaviour, Phillip's distress because of Sonia's behaviour, or both.

"Her parents owned a florist shop when she was growing up," I add, hoping some context might help soothe Phillip's hurt feelings.

"I know," Phillip responds. "She told me. She also told me my floral cooler was the wrong temperature, my arrangements were out of proportion, and she gave me a lesson in symmetry."

"Phillip, your floral arrangements are beautiful. Your proportions and symmetry are always perfect," I assure him, even though I'm not sure exactly what proportion and symmetry mean in the context of floral design.

"I know," Phillip concedes with less frustration and offense. "But it was hard to listen to her without defending myself."

"Why on earth didn't you defend yourself?" Connie asks.

"Because she's Sonia freaking Chang! The Pulitzer Prize-winning investigative reporter." He clears his throat. "I can barely say my own name in front of her. She's intimidating."

He's right, she is. Without saying a word, Sonia's mere silent presence can invoke an attack of self doubt. She's made of spectacular achievements and righteous confidence.

"There, there, Phillip," Connie comforts him and rubs his back. "Sonia will leave town in a few days. In the meantime, if you don't want to fill the order for her floral arrangement, don't. Let the Hendricks Agency find another florist to fill the order."

"And give her the satisfaction of intimidating me?" Phillip thrusts his chin into the air. "Never! I will create the most beautiful, proportioned, symmetrical floral arrangement the world has ever seen."

"You go, Phillip!

"Yes, you will!"

Connie and I cheer him on in unison as he leaves Knitorious.

"Wow," I say. "What do you think about that?"

"I think Phillip Wilde is the most talented florist I've ever met, regardless of Sonia Chang's opinion," Connie replies.

"I agree with you," I say. "Phillip is right about Sonia's tendency to take over. At my house, she insisted on arranging the flowers in a vase. She showed me the correct way to trim the stems and supervised while I did it. Her unapologetic assertiveness is one of the qualities that makes her so good at investigative journalism and television production."

"For someone as successful and controlling as Sonia Chang, it must've been difficult to accept that Rich fell in love with someone else, particularly someone Sonia regards as less accomplished than her." Connie makes a good point.

Could Sonia have intended to kill Emmy, but killed Armando instead? Or did Sonia kill Armando, then disclose his bigamy to give Emmy a motive for his murder? Not only would Sonia eliminate Emmy from *Hello, today!* and Rich Kendall's life, she would get accolades for uncovering Armando's bigamy and Emmy's motive.

"Why would Brad Hendricks send flowers to Sonia?" I wonder aloud. "Are they an item?"

"Who knows, my dear?" Connie shrugs. "But if they are, Sonia doesn't have a type, she has a spectrum. Brad and Rich are as different as two men can be."

She's right. Brad is intense and tenacious. He radiates competitiveness and ambition, and built his agency from scratch. Rich, on the other hand, is laid back and reactive. Thanks to his first-class private education, he's well-spoken and well-connected. He secured his audition for *Hello, today!* because he went to school with the son of the guy who runs the network.

Every instinct I have is tingling; something is going on between Brad and Sonia, and it goes deeper than dinner and flowers. If Armando's agent was dating Emmy's producer, Emmy would have told me. Whatever their situation is, it's a secret.

"Did you text Tina, my dear?" Connie asks, bringing me back to the here and now.

"Not yet," I reply. "I'll do it now."

I pull out my phone and send Tina a quick text.

While I have the text app open, I should text Adam. Maybe, as Emmy's lawyer, he can advise her not to return to work or give interviews while the police are investigating Armando's murder. My thumbs hover over the keyboard as I decide what to type. The bell over the door jingles.

"Hello, Megan."

"Hi, Mrs. Roblin. How are you?"

We go through the now-familiar exchange of pleas-antries. She asks me how Emmy is, I answer, and she asks me to pass along condolences on her behalf. While we banter, I abandon the unfinished text message to Adam, lock my phone, and slide it under the counter.

Mrs. Roblin is a member of Harmony Lake's Charity Knitting Guild, a collective of local knitters who use knitting to benefit worthy causes. The Charity Knitters, as we call them, are the driving force behind this month's Knitted Knocker campaign.

"How's Eric's problem?" Mrs. Roblin whispers, leaning over the counter.

I lean too, and we meet halfway, our foreheads only inches apart.

"Eric's problem?" I ask, confused. Then I remember the comment Phillip made about witch hazel, and I wonder if Mrs. Roblin is referring to the same thing. "I don't know what problem you mean, Mrs. Roblin."

Does Eric have a problem I don't know about?

"You know," Mrs. Roblin urges in a whisper. "His problem?" She winks and turns sideways, arching her back so her butt sticks out, then glances at it over her shoulder.

Why is she showing me her backside?

"I'm sorry, I don't know what you're talking about," I admit with a shrug.

Mrs. Roblin reaches into her large knitting bag and pulls out a blue, ring-shaped memory foam pillow. She slides it to me across the counter. Why is she offering me a hemorrhoid pillow?

"I was going to take it to the police station, but I

thought this would be more discreet. And I was coming here anyway, so it's more convenient."

"A hemorrhoid pillow?"

Mrs. Roblin replies with an understanding nod.

I squeeze my eyes shut tight when I realize what's happening. Word has gotten around about the hemorrhoid ointment Eric purchased on Sunday for Emmy's eyes.

"This is very thoughtful, Mrs. Roblin, but Eric doesn't need it." I nudge the doughnut-shaped cushion toward her. "He purchased the ointment for someone else." I smile.

"I see." Mrs. Roblin smiles at me again. "Perhaps *you* would like to borrow the pillow, Megan?" She slides it toward me again. "Keep it as long as necessary. I don't need it." She taps the cushion with her fingertips.

"The ointment wasn't for me, either," I explain, bumping the pillow toward her. "It was for my sister." Mrs. Roblin slides the pillow toward me again and opens her mouth to speak. I put my hand on the pillow and stop it mid-slide before it crosses the halfway point between us. "For her eyes," I add before she can offer the hemorrhoid pillow to Emmy.

"Her eyes?" Mrs. Roblin asks, flabbergasted.

I explain to Mrs. Roblin how people—TV people in particular, according to Emmy—sometimes use hemorrhoid cream to reduce swelling. Like when your eyes are swollen from crying because your husband died.

Excited about this potential new use for hemorrhoid

cream, Mrs. Roblin asks me if it would help her swollen ankles.

"I doubt it," I caution, hating to dampen her enthusiasm. "You should ask a medical professional before you apply it anywhere other than what the tube recommends."

"I'll go straight to the pharmacy after my shift and ask the pharmacist," Mrs. Roblin announces with glee.

"Your shift?" I ask.

"Yes, my shift," she reiterates. "I didn't just stop in to drop off the pillow. I'm here to help Connie watch the store so you can take care of your grieving sister and pursue your *hobby*." Mrs. Roblin opens her mouth and gives me an exaggerated wink.

My *hobby* is how The Charity Knitters refer to my propensity for sleuthing. They have taken it upon themselves to encourage and support my hobby because its inline with their aim of ensuring Harmony Lake remains the cozy, tight-knit, safe community we all know and love.

"I told her not to come in today, Verna, but she wouldn't listen," Connie chimes in, addressing Mrs. Roblin by her first name. "I told Megan the store would be fine without her, but she insisted on working today."

"We're short-staffed," I justify. "Marla is working at Artsy Tartsy until April gets back from…"

"Nonsense," Mrs. Roblin interrupts, joining me behind the counter and bumping me out of the way with her hip when she bends over to stuff her large knitting bag under the counter. "You're not short staffed. I'm here. Connie ran this store for almost forty years before you took over, Megan. I'm sure she can manage a few more days."

Mrs. Roblin flashes me a smile so sweet she might melt if she stepped outside in the rain.

There's no point fighting it, I'm overruled.

"Well, I was only working a half-day anyway, so I guess I can leave early."

It's not like I have a choice. I'm outnumbered, and they know when they join forces, I can't win.

"Take tomorrow off, too, my dear," Connie says, rubbing my arm. "Take care of Emmy."

"And every day after that until you finish your *hobby*," Mrs. Roblin adds with another indiscreet wink.

I collect my jacket and bag, then retrieve my phone from under the counter and text Adam.

Me: Can we meet? It's about Emmy.

Adam: I was going to text you the same thing. Can you come to my office?

Me: Law office or town hall?

Adam: Town Hall in forty-five minutes?

Me: I'll be there.

Harmony Lake Town Hall is a short walk from Knitorious. It would take longer to drive there and find parking than to walk. Also, it's not raining right now, and I can use some fresh air to clear my muddled thoughts.

I thank Connie and Mrs. Roblin for looking after Knitorious and remind them to call or text me if they need anything. Then, I leave through the front door and turn left, toward Latté Da. I have time to kill—pardon the pun—so I may as well get a chocolate caramel latté and savour it on my walk to the mayor's office.

As I approach Latté Da, a familiar, athletic figure lights a cigarette on the sidewalk outside the coffee shop. Brad Hendricks. Why is he at Latté Da? Is he satisfying a craving for the best coffee in the world, or is he posting his latest anti-Emmy blog post?

CHAPTER 21

"Megan!" Brad smiles.

"Brad!" I smile. "What brings you to the best coffee shop in the world?"

"This is my office today," he replies, holding his cigarette at arm's length and hugging me with his free arm. "I need to answer emails and stuff. The hotel is great, but their coffee is *meh*. I need good coffee, and I can work anywhere there's Wi-Fi."

The cigarette smoke ghosts a blue trail toward me, biting my nose and throat when I inhale.

"Smoke break?" I ask, nodding toward his cigarette.

"Yup. I reward myself with regular breaks. My laptop is inside." He jerks his thumb behind him. "How's Emmy doing?"

"Not great," I reply. "But she's strong. She'll be OK."

"How are you doing? You found him. That must be hard to deal with."

"It is. But I'll be OK too. I have a lot of support," I reply. "How are you?"

"I have to stop myself from texting him about ten times a day," Brad says, his voice thick with emotion. "I have to take calls, and answer emails, and act like everything is normal, and my best friend didn't die two days ago."

"I'm sorry for your loss," I say.

"Ditto."

"I was just talking about you this morning," I say, changing the subject.

"Good things I hope?" Brad gives me a wink and a sideways grin.

"My neighbour, the florist, was filling an order for The Hendricks Agency," I say, watching Brad's face for a reaction. Nothing.

"I guess what they say about small town gossip is true," Brad chortles, taking a drag off his cigarette and exhaling a cloud of white smoke.

"We're more tight-knit than you city-folk are used to," I say, playing along. "Which lucky lady will receive one of Phillip's gorgeous floral arrangements?"

"It's not what you think," Brad chuckles. "A client and his wife had a baby."

He's lying with a straight face while looking me in the eye. No fidgeting, no sweating. He takes another drag of his cigarette without breaking eye contact.

"I thought they might be for someone special." I smile.

"Megan, if you're asking if I'm available, the answer is yes." Brad puts his hands on the wall behind me, trapping me, then narrows his eyes and brings his face closer until we're almost nose-to-nose. He reeks of stale cigarettes and coffee. "I thought you were wrapped up tight in Chief Sloane's long arm of the law," he says in a low, husky voice. "But I'll be in town for a few more days if you want to get together."

He's uncomfortably close. Being pinned between his ego and the wall is making me claustrophobic. Brad moves his hand to bring his cigarette to his mouth, and I duck out of his man-made cage, retreating to a safe distance. He turns to face me, leaning his back against the wall and flicking cigarette ash onto the sidewalk.

"No, thanks," I sneer. "I don't mess around, and you're not my type."

"It was a joke, Megan!" Brad's awkward laugh doesn't conceal his wounded pride. "I was kidding." He exaggerates his words and shrugs with his hands facing the sky. "But for real, Chief Sloane is a lucky man. I apologize if you thought I was serious. To be honest, I haven't been myself since Armando died."

He drops his cigarette butt on the sidewalk. "The police are still at the hotel, and Sloane keeps asking me questions. The same questions over and over. It's making me paranoid. He acts like he doesn't believe me, and he's trying to catch me in a lie."

He rubs the ball of his foot on the cigarette butt.

"*Will* he catch you in a lie?" I ask.

"Of course not," Brad retorts, bending down to pick up the flattened cigarette butt and lobbing it into a nearby trash can. "Anyway, I lawyered up. Your fiancé can't question me anymore unless my lawyer is present."

"Then why are you paranoid?"

"I returned to my room around the time Armando died," Brad reveals. "The keycard keeps a record every time I unlock the door. Eric kept asking if I saw anyone or anything strange near Armando's room when I entered my room."

"Did you?"

"No," Brad shrugs. "I turned right off the elevator. Armando's room is left. I didn't look left. I saw nothing."

"Where were you before you returned to your room?" I ask.

"Gym," Brad replies. "But there's no proof. Another guest used his keycard to unlock the door and held it open for me." He shoves his hands in his pants pockets. "My lawyer says my alibi is weak."

"The guest who let you in can confirm it," I suggest.

"I used the weight room, and he used the sauna. We didn't see each other again."

"And because you didn't need your keycard to *leave* the gym, you can't prove how long you were there," I deduce.

"Right," Brad says. "And there aren't a lot of security cameras at the hotel. Which, ironically, was one reason I booked it. Privacy was important to Armando, and he didn't like hotels that record his every move."

"Armando was your best friend," I say, summoning my most sympathetic voice. "I'm sure if you had *any* information, *any at all*, you'd tell the police. Because you want to find your best friend's killer just as much as they do, right?"

"Yeah,"—Brad shrugs one shoulder—"of course I

would. But they don't need to know *everything*. Like they don't need to know about something that won't help them. Like small insignificant stuff that has nothing to do with Armando's death."

I get the sense Brad didn't tell the police the whole truth about the morning Armando died.

"Sometimes, information that seems insignificant is important. Eric says they solve cases all the time because of a small, seemingly insignificant tip." I pause. Brad's eyes dart left and right like a trapped animal looking for an escape route. "What's insignificant to you could be the key to putting Armando's killer behind bars."

"Megan, if I tell you something, will you tell me if you think it's significant?"

"Of course. Armando was my brother-in-law. I want justice for him as much as you."

"The night before he died, I texted Armando about going to the gym in the morning. He didn't text me back. I wasn't surprised. Emmy was there, and I figured he was taking time away from his phone." Perspiration beads on Brad's forehead. "The next morning, when Armando still hadn't replied to my text, I left for the gym without him. While I was waiting for the elevator, I heard a knock. Someone from room service was knocking on Armando's door. The door to Armando's room opened just as I stepped onto the elevator."

"Did you see Armando open the door?" I ask.

"No, but the lady who delivered the food said, 'Good morning, Mr. Garcia,' and I heard Armando say, 'Good morning' as the elevator door closed."

Didn't Eric say the room service employee who delivered Armando's food was a man?

"You heard a woman's voice, then Armando's voice," I confirm.

"Right."

"Would you recognize her if you saw her again?"

"I think so," Brad replies with a one-shoulder shrug.

"Why didn't you tell the police?"

"Because of what happened next," Brad looks at his feet, embarrassed. "After the gym, I returned to my room and had a shower. Then I texted Armando again. He read the text but didn't reply. He left me on read, Megan. My best friend left me on read!"

According to my twenty-year-old daughter, Hannah, leaving someone *on read* is rude and a major breach of online etiquette. *On read* means you read the text message but didn't reply.

"You thought Armando was ignoring you?"

"It's the only logical conclusion, right?!" Brad smiles, and his face relaxes with relief.

He interprets my question as validation of his frustration, not as the confirmation of fact that I intended it to be.

If Brad's ego is as fragile as it is enormous, being ignored by Armando would have angered and offended him. Was Brad angry and offended enough to kill Armando?

"What did you do about it?" I ask. "You didn't let Armando ignore you and not *do* anything, right?"

I continue to sympathize, hoping Brad will continue to confide more details.

"I went to his room again," Brad replies, vindicated.

"You were inside Armando's hotel room on Sunday morning?" I ask, trying to hide my shock.

"No." Brad replies. "I knocked, but Armando didn't answer the door." He shifts his weight from one foot to the other, and beads of sweat form on his upper lip. "I knocked again and shouted, 'Hey buddy! It's me. Open the door.'"

"Did Armando open the door?"

Brad shakes his head, and his dark eyes fill with moisture.

"I should've kept knocking," Brad says, then swallows hard. "I shouldn't have left. Maybe if I forced him to answer, Armando would still be alive. But I was mad. I thought he was ignoring me. I thought he and Emmy were in there laughing at me. I stomped down the hall to my room."

"I don't think Armando was ignoring you," I say. "Emmy wasn't there, she was at brunch with me. It's possible, when you knocked, Armando was already dead."

"He wasn't dead, Megan," Brad says matter-of-factly. "He read my text message a few minutes before."

"Maybe he was debilitated and unable to answer the door," I suggest.

"Then why did he open it to hang the DO NOT DISTURB sign?"

"You saw Armando open the door and hang the sign?"

"No, I was walking back to my room when I heard a door open and close. I knew it was Armando's door. I stomped back to Armando's room, and he'd hung the DO NOT DISTURB sign on the door."

"And it wasn't there before?" I confirm.

Brad shakes his head.

"The sign was still swinging."

A shiver runs along my spine when I imagine Armando's killer's hand hanging the DO NOT DISTURB sign on his door.

CHAPTER 22

ADAM FLARES his nostrils and twitches his nose.

"Meg, have you been smoking?" he asks, closing his office door and pausing on the way to his desk to sniff around me.

"You know I don't smoke," I reply. "Brad Hendricks smokes, and I was just with him."

"What were you doing with *Brad Hendricks*?" Adam asks, pronouncing Brad's name with a scornful inflection.

"Getting lied to," I respond, laying my jacket over the back of the chair in the mayor's office.

"Be careful around him, Meg. He's a lech."

Adam sits behind his desk and leans back, resting his ankle on his opposite knee and swiveling his chair in lazy semicircles.

"You've only met him twice. How do you know he's a lech?"

"Remember Emmy and Armando's reception? Brad asked me if I knew you and if you were single." Adam rolls his eyes. "Even after I told him I was your husband, he kept looking at you like your dress was filet mignon."

"You never told me that," I say.

"I forgot about it until I saw him at Latté Da earlier."

"Anyway," I say, directing the conversation to the reason for our meeting. "Rumour has it, Emmy is returning to work tomorrow. A segment for *Hello, today!* because they want to capitalize on the increased viewership Monday's show had."

Adam sighs. "It's not a good idea, Meg. Emmy shouldn't make any public statements or answer questions. Armando's death is an active murder investigation. She could say something to implicate herself."

"I know. That's why I'm here," I say. "I'm hoping that, as her lawyer, you'll help me convince her it's a bad idea." I shake my head and huff. "I can't believe they'd exploit Emmy's grief to increase their ratings."

"Emmy knows the score," Adam asserts. "She's grieving, Meg, but your sister is smart, and she's been in the industry a long time. She knows they want to increase ratings and lure new viewers to the show. If Emmy agreed to do it, she knows what she agreed to. It's not in her best interest, and I'll tell her that, but she's not as naïve as you think."

"But she's grieving, and maybe she's not thinking straight. Someone has to look out for her. And by someone, I mean us. I'm her sister, and you're her lawyer."

"Speaking of looking out for Emmy," Adam segues, opening a file folder on his desk. "Sonia told you the truth. Armando Garcia was already married when he married Emmy. There's no record of his first marriage ending in divorce, death, or annulment. He was still married to the first Mrs. Garcia when he died."

"This will break Emmy's heart, Adam," I say, on the verge of tears.

"There's more," he says, stone-faced. "The first Mrs. Garcia has three children, and Armando's name is on the birth certificates as their father."

"Armando had kids?"

I'm gobsmacked. My mouth hangs ajar, speechless.

"The youngest is three years old."

"How is that possible?" I demand. "Armando hasn't returned to Ecuador since he left fifteen years ago." I pause while a thought occurs to me. "Unless she comes here…"

Adam raises his hands off his desk, then lowers them again in a calm-down gesture, interrupting my train of thought.

"We won't mention the kids yet," he says. "We should tell Emmy about Armando's first wife, but I don't think we should mention the potential kids. Just because his name is on the birth certificates, doesn't mean he's the biological father."

"What about the rest of Armando's family?"

"Nothing as exciting," Adam replies, flipping through the pages in the open file folder. "His parents live in Ecuador. They previously lived in Brazil and Columbia. Emmy was right about Armando having a sister. Her name is Cristina Garcia. She emigrated years ago. I couldn't find anything else about her. She probably got married and changed her last name. And the best friend Emmy mentioned, who was like a brother to Armando, kind of *was* Armando's brother. His name is Mateo Cruz. Mateo's parents died in a single-vehicle car accident when he was eleven. Mateo was the only survivor. The Cruz family and the Garcia family were friends, and Armando's parents became Mateo's legal guardians. I haven't found any information about Mateo Cruz's life after the Garcias became his legal guardians."

"Anything else?" I ask. "I'd like to get the shock over with at once."

HELLO, world! Guess who's making a comeback?

Rumour has it our favourite mourning show host is plotting a comeback this week. We knew she'd come out from under the mountain of casserole dishes and condolence flowers, eventually. Her smitten co-host is thrilled. He can't wait to have her on the sofa again! Meanwhile, the grieving widow's crafty sister has been knotty! She and a certain sports agent got up close and personal outside a trendy café. Was he whispering sweet nothings in her ear or just blowing smoke? Was she needling him for information about a certain soccer player's last kick at the ball?

"Uggggghhhh," I groan, when April finishes reading the disgraceful drivel. "The double entendres are horrendous!"

"I know, right?!" April agrees. "I cringed when I read it."

"When was it posted?" I ask.

"A few minutes ago," April replies. "I subscribed to the stupid blog, so I'll get notified whenever they publish a new post."

"Can you send me the link?"

I'm in the car, on my way home from Adam's office. April called me to tell me about the mystery blogger's latest post.

"What were you and Brad doing outside Latté Da?" April asks. "The blog implies you and Brad were... cozy."

I tell April about Brad pinning me against the wall.

"The mystery blogger misinterpreted the situation," I add.

"What a creep!" April exclaims.

I'm not sure if she means Brad or the mystery blogger, but the descriptor applies to both.

"Brad must be the mystery blogger," I surmise. "Who else could it be?"

"How would Brad Hendricks know about Emmy returning to work?" April asks.

"Sonia!"

I tell April about the flower order for Sonia from Brad's agency.

"Talk about strange bedfellows," she says. "If Brad and Sonia are an item, why did he make you an indecent proposal?"

So many questions, so few answers.

"WHERE'S POPPY?" I ask, crouching down to greet Sophie.

"She went to Harmony Hills to get a new phone. She destroyed hers."

"What happened to it?"

"She was doing my laundry and somehow dropped her phone in the load of darks," Emmy says, sitting sideways with her knees slung over the arm of the chair, leafing through a bridal magazine. "She spent all morning searching for it. I found it when I helped her fold the laundry."

"You let Poppy do your laundry?" I ask, wondering if laundry is a PA task or a best friend task.

"I don't *let* her do it. She wants to do it." Emmy shrugs. "She just *does* it. Poppy's always auditing my life, searching for things to fix. Today she fixed my laundry situation." She raises her index finger. "Technically, she did *your* laundry since I've been wearing your clothes since Sunday."

Emmy closes the magazine and adds it to the pile on the floor next to the chair.

"The closest phone store is in Harmony Hills," I say.

"She knows," Emmy says. "She looked it up on my phone. The good news is, Poppy's phone was insured. She gets an identical replacement, and it won't cost her anything."

Reaching for Sophie's leash, I spy a familiar to-go cup on the kitchen counter. "Did you go out today?"

"I sat in the car while Poppy ran into Latté Da," Emmy replies. "Their pumpkin spice is addictive."

I'm glad Emmy left the house and drank something without being nagged into submission.

"Adam's coming over. He wants to talk to you. I texted you, but you didn't reply." I say, attaching Sophie's leash.

"Sorry," Emmy says. "I gave Poppy my phone to ease her anxiety about not having one. And I didn't want her to drive all the way to Harmony Hills without one."

"Poppy knows the password to unlock your phone?"

"Sometimes Poppy needs to access my phone for work," Emmy explains, picking up the pile of magazines.

"I'm taking Sophie for a walk before Adam gets here."

Eric's car pulls into the driveway as Sophie and I step outside. We wait for him at the top of the driveway. Sophie tippy-taps her front paws, excited to greet him. Me too, Sophie, me too.

"Hey, handsome."

"Want some company?" Eric asks, getting out of his car.

We meander down the street hand-in-hand, stopping at trees, fire hydrants, and wherever else Sophie's nose dictates.

"How's your day?" I ask.

"Weird," Eric says, rubbing the back of his neck. "People keep asking how I'm feeling. They look at me like they pity me. Two people suggested I try witch hazel, and a third asked me if I've had a bath with

Epsom salts. I told them I didn't know what they were talking about, but they just smiled and nodded. The desk sergeant switched chairs with me because his chair is softer and better for my problem. What problem? Babe, I don't know what they're talking about."

"They're talking about your heinie, honey," I say, giving it a discreet tap.

I explain to Eric how word spread about the hemorrhoid cream he purchased for Emmy.

He doubles over laughing so hard he grabs his stomach because it hurts.

"I bought three tubes!" He says between fits of laughter. "I didn't know what brand to get." He wipes tears from his eyes. "Everyone must think my hemorrhoid situation is pretty serious."

"Connie and Mrs. Roblin know the truth," I tell him. "I assured them your derriere is perfect. Word should spread through the rest of the town by tonight."

"I guess my backside being the *butt* of local gossip is a hazard of living in a small, tight-knit community." His amusement at his own pun triggers a laughter aftershock.

Eric's butt pun reminds me of today's blog post.

"There's another blog post," I say.

"I know," Eric responds. "You talked to Brad Hendricks."

"Yes," I confirm. "But it wasn't as intimate as the blog post suggests."

I tell Eric about my interaction with Brad, including the part where he trapped me between him and the wall.

"Did any part of him touch any part of you?" Eric asks, his jaw clenching and unclenching.

"No," I assure him. "He only trapped me for a few seconds. The blogger just had perfect timing."

"I need to show Brad a photo lineup of employees who worked at Rise & Glide on Sunday. With any luck, he'll recognize the woman he saw delivering food to Armando's room. While he's there, I'll pin him against a wall and talk to him about personal space and respect."

"I don't know if I believe his story," I say. "Lying comes easy to Brad. When he lied about the flowers he ordered for Sonia, he didn't fidget, blink, twitch, or break eye contact. If I didn't know for a fact that the flowers were for Sonia, I would've believed his lie."

"The cigarette package we found in Armando's room and the butts on the balcony belong to Brad," Eric says. "Forensics confirmed Brad's DNA was the only DNA present on them."

"DNA doesn't prove *when* Brad was in Armando's room," I point out. "He admits he was there on Saturday, but no one noticed the cigarette butts or empty cigarette pack until Sunday. We only have Brad's word for when he was inside the room. And he's already lied at least once."

"Deb confirmed that Armando declined housekeeping services when he checked in, and there's no record of him requesting anything that housekeeping would have delivered to his room."

"Then why did housekeeping enter his room on Saturday morning?" I ask.

"I've interviewed the housekeeping employees, and they deny being in his room."

"Great, another mystery to solve."

"We know how the drugs got into Armando's system," Eric says.

"How?"

"The killer drugged the food on the room service cart."

"Does that mean you suspect the employee who delivered the food? Or whoever prepared the food?"

"I wish it were that easy," Eric says with a sigh. "Armando followed a strict eating plan that required him to eat specific foods at specific times. He gave a copy to the hotel when he checked in on Friday. The chef posted it on the kitchen wall. Some items on Armando's eating plan aren't foods the hotel typically stocks. They brought in food just for him. They segregated it, labelled with his name and room number. Anyone who had access to the kitchen had access to the food. They'd know which food was Armando's and even when each item would be prepared and delivered to him."

I flashback to when Deb escorted Emmy and me out of the hotel through the delivery entrance.

"The delivery entrance is by the kitchen," I say. "When we left the hotel on Sunday, Deb took Emmy and I to the delivery entrance. The kitchen is right there. The punch clock is right there. Employees were coming and going from their shifts, and employees who were on their breaks were socializing just outside the delivery entrance. Anyone could have accessed Armando's food."

"Even someone who doesn't work there, like delivery people," Eric adds. "And when the weather is nice, they leave the door open for fresh air."

"This eliminates Emmy as a suspect, right?"

"The food arrived after you and Emmy left for brunch. Since Emmy didn't have access to the food to tamper with it, she can't be the murderer."

"That's amazing!" I stand on my tippy toes, throw my arms around his neck, and give him a kiss. "I'm so relieved. We can tell Emmy, right? As soon as we get home?"

"Absolutely!"

"This might make it easier for Emmy to hear the news about Armando's first wife," I hope aloud.

"The cyber unit found the source of the second blog post."

"The one posted on Sunday?" I ask. "About Armando's death?"

"It was posted from Emmy's phone."

I sigh and nod, unsurprised.

"Of course, it was," I mutter, rolling my eyes and shaking my head.

"Babe, are you sure Emmy didn't go to Latté Da on Sunday? She didn't have to go inside. She could've picked up the Wi-Fi signal from the parking lot or the sidewalk."

"I can guarantee Emmy wasn't anywhere near Latté Da on Sunday, but I can't say the same about her phone."

CHAPTER 23

"IT'S A SILENT MONTAGE," Emmy pleads. "I won't even wear a mic. The camera crew will get footage of me looking forlorn. They'll edit the footage so it captures the essence of my grief. Now that Eric has eliminated me as a suspect, I don't have to worry about incriminating myself."

"They're using you to increase ratings," Adam points out.

"And I'm using them to counteract the negative publicity I've gotten since Armando died."

"What negative publicity?" Adam asks.

"I'll text you links," Eric replies, referring to the gossip blog.

"That gossip blog makes me seem like a merry widow, and when the media covers Armando's death, they use photos of Armando and I smiling and laughing. The world needs to see that I'm a real person and my grief is real."

"You know about the gossip blog?" I ask.

"*You* know about the gossip blog?" Emmy retorts.

"I found it by accident on Sunday. How did you find out?"

"People told me," Emmy replies with a shrug.

"You weren't supposed to find out," I say. "We didn't want you to stress about it."

"We?" Emmy asks.

"Poppy and April and me," I reply. "April monitors the blog and tells me about new posts. Poppy offered to contact the blog and ask them to remove the posts."

Emmy chuckles. "Poppy didn't contact them, did she?"

"She forgot," I reply. "The last few days have been overwhelming. I'm not surprised she forgot. But they deleted the posts, anyway. How do you know Poppy didn't contact them?"

"Poppy is the most non-confrontational person I know," Emmy replies. "She doesn't even send back food at a restaurant when they give her the wrong order. Sending a cease-and-desist letter would be way outside her comfort zone. The blog deleted the posts because *I* contacted them."

"There's something else we need to talk to you about," I say. "Did you and Armando ever talk about your previous marriages?"

"Of course," Emmy replies. "He knew about both of my previous marriages."

"How about Armando?" Adam asks. "Was he ever married before you?"

"No," Emmy insists. "He was too focused on his career to have a serious relationship."

"Armando was married to someone else before he married you," I state.

"Who told you this lie?" Emmy demands, crossing her arms in front of her chest and arranging her legs in an aristocratic leg cross.

She bounces her foot in the air.

"Sonia Chang," I reply.

"Lies!" Emmy rolls her eyes, bouncing her foot harder and faster. "Sonia hates me. She's been trying to get rid of me since the day they hired me."

"She has proof."

"Fake!"

"I verified it, Emmy," Adam adds. "It's true."

"I verified it too," Eric says. "As part of the investigation. Adam and I came to the same conclusion as Sonia."

"Fine!" Emmy shrugs one shoulder. "So what? Armando was divorced and didn't tell me. Big deal. It changes nothing."

"He wasn't divorced," I say. "Armando was still married to his first wife when he died."

Emmy lets out a gasp like someone punched her in the gut. She looks from me to Adam to Eric, searching for a hint of doubt. We're all steadfast and certain.

"Sonia must love this," she scoffs. "I bet that smug, arrogant witch couldn't wait to tell you."

Emmy's face flushes with angry heat.

"It's not about her, Emmy," Eric says.

"Why was Sonia looking into Armando's past, anyway?" Emmy asks.

"She said she was following an unrelated tip, and somehow it led to him. She wouldn't elaborate," I say.

"There was no other tip," Emmy concludes with a huff. "I bet she looked for something scandalous in my past, but my life's an open book. When she couldn't find anything to destroy me, she went after Armando. No wonder she won a Pulitzer." Emmy scoffs. "Show me the proof."

I watch Adam pass the file folder on his lap to Emmy, hoping he removed the birth certificates.

As Emmy flips through the pages, inspecting each one, her demeanour weakens from hostile denial to broken sadness.

"You guys know his sister's name, his best friend's name, his parents' names... you know Armando better after three days than I did after three years." She closes the file and drops it on the coffee table. "My husband was a stranger."

"This doesn't change how you felt about each other," Eric reminds her. "It doesn't change that Armando loved you and you love him."

"I'm not even his widow, a woman in South America is." Emmy swallows hard, choking back tears, and dabbing her eyes with the cuff of her—my—half-button chambray shirt. "There's no way I'm doing the grief montage for *Hello, to*day!" She shakes her head with angry determination. "Not anymore. Where's my phone?" Emmy scans the room for her phone.

"Poppy has it," I remind her.

"I need it," Emmy says. "I need to call them and tell them I won't be filming tomorrow. The contact information is in my phone. I need Poppy to bring back my phone."

"I'll pick it up for you," I offer.

It's time to confront the non-confrontational Poppy and shove her outside her comfort zone.

ROOM 204... 206... 208. I take a deep breath and remind myself to stay calm. Heavy shoulders, long arms. One more deep breath. I knock on the door.

"Hey, Megan!"

I force a smile.

"Hi, Poppy."

She stands aside so I can enter the small motel room.

"Where's Emmy?"

"At home."

"Who's with her?"

Poppy's forehead corrugates with worry. Is her concern authentic? Since learning Poppy Prescott isn't who I thought she was, I'm not sure if anything she says or does is genuine.

"Eric," I reply. "Emmy needs her phone. I'm here to pick it up."

"Sure thing," Poppy says, unplugging Emmy's phone from the nightstand between the two double beds. "Tell her I said thank you."

She extends the phone toward me.

"Did you publish the blog post when you were at Latté Da with Emmy or when you went to get your new phone?" I ask, snatching the phone from Poppy's hand.

"W-what blog post?"

"Today's blog post," I specify. "I get why you're confused since you post so many. This was your third one since Saturday, right?"

"What are you talking about?" Poppy screws up her face in confusion and lets out a nervous half-laugh.

"You're the mystery blogger."

"What?" Poppy asks, her brown eyes wide. "Why would you think that?"

"Where should I start?" I jab my fists into my hips and jut out my neck with righteous indignation. "The mystery blogger followed Emmy to Harmony Lake. You followed Emmy to Harmony Lake. The first blog post, about Emmy and Armando's marital problems, was published at a coffee shop near Emmy's house before you left for Harmony Lake. The second post, about Armando's death, was published at Latté Da using Emmy's phone. Except Emmy wasn't anywhere near Latté Da on Sunday. But her phone was."

"How did Emmy's phone go to Latté Da without her?" Poppy asks.

"You took it," I reply. "You stayed with Emmy in the guest room until she fell asleep. Then, when you left to pick up her essentials, you took her phone with you. You returned it when you got back. You used Emmy's phone to frame her as the mystery blogger. When I told you about the first blog post, you pretended not to know about it. But your eyes filled with fear when I told you the police were looking into it. Then, when we discussed the second blog post, you asked me if the police would be able to find the blogger's location *and* device. You panicked when I told you they might locate the device. You panicked so much that you destroyed your phone and replaced it with an identical one." I point to Poppy's phone on the nightstand. "You put your phone in the laundry and told Emmy you lost it. You were planning to tell Emmy you found your phone when you got the new, identical replacement. But Emmy thwarted your plan when she found your old phone in the laundry. If your plan had worked, when the police traced the blog to your phone, you would've tried to deny it by giving them your new phone and claiming you couldn't be the blogger. Today, you published another blog post from Latté Da using Emmy's phone, ensuring the finger of suspicion would point at her instead of you."

"I wasn't at Latté Da today," Poppy insists. "I was at your house with Emmy. Then I went to Harmony Hills to get a new phone."

"Yes, you were. Emmy waited in the car while you went in. The cup from her pumpkin spice coffee is still in the kitchen. You saw Brad and I on the sidewalk outside."

"Does Emmy know?" Poppy asks, defeated and lowering herself to sit on the edge of the bed.

"I don't know. I think she might," I reply. "I suspected it was you when she told me you knew her password, but something she said made me certain."

"What did she say?"

"She said you're the most non-confrontational person she knows," I say, quoting Emmy. "It made me realize the blogger is a coward. Only a coward would say such hateful, cruel things and hide behind the anonymity of the internet. The other people I suspected are too direct and opinionated to hide their hate behind an anonymous blog post. They prefer to hate Emmy honestly and in the open."

"Please don't tell her," Poppy pleads, pressing her palms together.

"Why did you do it?" I ask, ignoring her plea. "Do you hate Emmy?"

"I love Emmy. She's my best friend," Poppy explains. "But sometimes I get... frustrated at how entitled she is and how much adoration she gets. Don't tell me you don't see it, Megan. Like after Armando died, Emmy worried about what people would say about her puffy eyes. She freaked out when I couldn't find the right brand of moisturizer because she doesn't want her skin to breakout while she's in mourning. She had a gorgeous husband who worshipped her, but she played head games with him and made him chase her across the country to prove it. Men trip over themselves to get any attention from her. Rich Kendall has been in love with her for years, and his constant attention annoys her. Big companies rush products to your house with overnight delivery just so she'll keep using their stuff. It's like the world revolves around her, and she expects it to."

"She didn't deserve the vitriol you posted about her, Poppy. Or to be framed for it."

"I know. You're right."

"What about the other posts? The non-Emmy posts. Did you write those too?"

Poppy nods. "Do you know what my superpower is?"

"Bad puns?"

"My other superpower," she chuckles. "Invisibility. People don't notice me. I blend into the background. People talk like I'm not in the room. It doesn't occur to them that I'm listening. And even when they notice me, it's a matter of time before they get used to my presence and act like I'm not there. I hear a lot of stuff, Megan. A LOT. I need to put it somewhere. Do something with it. The gossip blog is my outlet. I leave the other posts, but I delete the posts about Emmy because I love her. I posted them when I was angry or frustrated, but when the feeling passed, I deleted them."

"Not because she sent you a cease-and-desist email?"

"I get those all the time." Poppy flicks her wrist. "I ignore them."

This explains why, as April pointed out, the blog focuses on people related to the network that airs *Hello, today!* and the cast members of *Perfect Match*. Poppy works there. She's in the building every day.

"Do the police know I'm the mystery blogger?"

"I asked Eric to let me talk to you first. I can't make any promises, but I'll ask him to consider this a private matter if you help me."

"Anything."

"First, delete today's blog post about Emmy."

"Already done," Poppy says. "I deleted it about an hour ago. And I promise I won't write anymore gossip posts about Emmy."

"Next, what's the deal with Brad Hendricks and Sonia Chang?"

"They dated for a while on the down low," Poppy replies. "I got the feeling Brad was more into Sonia than Sonia was into him. I think she used him for his physical attributes, if you know what I mean, and hoped he would make Rich jealous. It didn't work. Rich only has eyes for Emmy.

"Past tense? They aren't together anymore?"

"Sonia ended it about two weeks ago. Brad didn't take it well. He even showed up at the station to see her. Sonia didn't like that. She told him if he came to the station again, she'd get security to escort him out. She hates attention unless it's attention for how good she is at her job. Sonia is always secretive, but for the past couple of weeks, she's been more secretive than usual. I noticed she started carrying a second phone and disappears when it rings."

"Does Sonia smoke?" I ask.

"No. Definitely not. Sonia's a health nut. Her entire life is a practice in control and discipline. She follows a strict diet and exercise plan and says smoking is pollution for the body."

Sonia had a faint aroma of cigarette smoke when she was at my house on Monday and said she knew what Brad said about *Perfect Match* devaluing the Armando Garcia brand. He made that comment to Armando on Thursday. How did Sonia hear about it? Emmy didn't tell her. It had to be Brad. If Sonia hates smoking, why was she dating him? Is Brad her source? Did he tell her about Armando's first wife? Did Sonia date Brad to use him for information about Emmy and Armando?

"Where's Emmy?" I ask Eric, who's hunched over the coffee table typing on his laptop, surrounded by papers.

"Bathtub," he replies. "She said you're out of Himalayan bath salts."

"Because she uses them every day," I grumble, dropping my tired self onto the sofa next to him.

"How did it go with Poppy?" Eric asks, leaning back.

"As we expected," I reply, then tell him about our illuminating conversation.

"At least we can cross one mystery off the list," Eric says. "Do you think Poppy killed Armando?"

"No," I say, shaking my head. "What motive would she have?"

Sophie jumps up and nestles between us.

"What motive did she have for the blog posts?" Eric asks, answering my question with another question.

"Frustration. Jealousy. But I don't think she's frustrated or jealous enough to kill Armando. Her goal with the blog is to vent, not to hurt anyone. That's why she doesn't use names, and that's why she deleted the posts about Emmy. Poppy promised she wouldn't write anymore anti-Emmy blog posts."

"Will you tell Emmy that Poppy is the mystery blogger?"

"I think so." I nod. "I suspect she knows, but I'll tell her, anyway."

"Do you think it'll ruin their friendship, babe?"

I shrug. "That's up to them."

"Did you learn anything else?"

"Sonia and Brad were dating. I don't know how long they were together, but it was hush-hush, and she ended it two weeks ago."

The coroner's report is open on Eric's laptop.

"Do you know where the killer got the Rohypnol and the Fentanyl?" I ask.

"They're common street drugs," Eric replies. "The killer could've gotten them anywhere. But they had to get them in advance. And plan how and when to contaminate Armando's food. This is a premeditated murder, not a crime of opportunity. The killer had to arrange everything ahead of time."

"Revenge," I suggest, eyeing the coroner's report. "The killer–or killers–had time to let their anger fester and plot their revenge."

"We released the crime scene," Eric says. "Emmy can pick up her stuff whenever she wants."

"Did you tell Emmy already?"

Eric nods. "She wants to go in the morning. Let me know if you need help. I have to go to Rise & Glide anyway to interview employees."

"Did you interview the person who delivered Armando's food?"

"He's still sick," Eric replies. "Deb said he got dehydrated and needed IV fluids."

"I guess gut rot isn't as fast as Tina says it is."

"Tina?" Eric asks. "The knitter?"

"She had gut rot on Sunday and Monday. She said it was an intense twenty-four-hour bug."

"Tina works at Rise & Glide?" Eric asks. "I don't remember seeing anyone named Tina on the employee list," Eric says, leaning forward and picking up a file folder. He scans the first page, then the second. "No Tina."

"She said she left before we found Armando's body. Maybe she's not on the list because she left early."

"If that's the case, this list is incomplete and there are more employees to interview." Eric exhales a tired sigh. "I need to interview every employee who worked between Friday and Sunday. Not just employees who worked on Sunday."

"Sorry, honey."

"I'll ask Deb about it in the morning," Eric says, making a note inside the file folder.

"May I look at the coroner's report?"

"Go ahead," Eric says, handing me his laptop.

"It says here that Armando previously fractured his clavicle and previously fractured his distal radius," I comment. "Emmy never mentioned it."

"The coroner estimates the fractures were over twenty years old. They've long since healed," Eric says, scrolling through the report. "It says here,"—Eric points to the screen—"that the previous fractures are not relevant to the cause of death."

"It also says the coroner estimates the fractures happened at the same time. How did Armando break his collarbone and his wrist at the same time?"

"The coroner said the older the fracture, the harder it is to pinpoint the exact timeframe," Eric explains. "The coroner's time frame is an estimate. But he was close. According to the medical history his team doctors gave me, Armando told them he fell out of a tree and broke his collarbone at age ten, and fell off a bike and broke his wrist at age twelve."

"Armando was lucky he didn't break something that impacted his soccer career like his friend Mateo's career-ending knee injury," I say.

No wonder Mateo was jealous when Armando made the major leagues and he didn't.

CHAPTER 24

"Hi, Deb," I call out, approaching her from behind.

"Hello, Megan!" Deb excuses herself from the landscaper she's talking to and walks toward us with Blitz and Abby leading the way. She gives me a hug. "If you're looking for Eric, he's not here yet. I'm expecting him in about an hour."

"Actually, we're looking for you," I say, handing her a bouquet. "We wanted to thank you for everything you did on Sunday."

"Oh, my." Deb blushes, taking the flowers. "You shouldn't have. I didn't do anything. I wish I could've done more."

"You helped us through a horrible situation," I insist. "You took care of Emmy and me when we were in shock."

Emmy thanks Deb and gives her a hug. They both tear up and apologize to each other for the awful events of the previous Sunday that were neither woman's fault.

"Thank you! I'll go straight inside and put them in my office."

"We'll walk in with you," I say. "We're collecting Emmy's things from Room 814."

"I'll send a porter to help you," Deb offers.

"Thanks," I reply, squinting into the morning sun. "Is Tina working? She left her jacket at Knitorious yesterday, and I brought it with me."

"She's coming in late," Deb explains. "I don't know if you heard, but one of our employees got the gut rot real bad. He had to go to the hospital. Well, Tina is visiting him today and taking him a thermos of soup. I told her she could come in late. You can leave her jacket with me. I'll be sure she gets it."

"I'll go get it," Emmy offers.

I hand Emmy the car keys and tell her Tina's jacket is in the backseat.

"Tina has nominated herself as Gary's caregiver," Deb continues.

"Gary?"

"The employee who got the gut rot real bad."

"Right."

"I think she feels responsible for him since she saved his life."

"Tina saved Gary's life?" I ask. "How?"

"She found him and got him to the hospital. He was dehydrated and needed IV fluids," Deb explains. "Gary lives alone, and Tina lives nearby. She stopped by to check on him. She said he was weak and pale and confused. She took him to the hospital. He's home now, but he's still sick, and she's taken it upon herself to check on him every day."

"Tina's very thoughtful," I agree. "I hope Gary makes a full recovery and returns to work soon."

"YOU DON'T HAVE to go in," I say, looking at the numbers on the door and bracing myself to return to the scene of the crime. "You can wait in the car. I'll get everything and meet you there."

"I'm doing it," Emmy says, staring at the door handle like she's trying to open it with telepathy.

I've offered to collect her things at least half a dozen times since last night, but Emmy wants to be here. "Ready?"

"Ready."

Emmy swipes the card and opens the door. The room is bright with daylight, unlike last time we were here. I'm flooded by emotions when I step inside. Somehow it feels like a different room and the same room, all at once. It feels like we found Armando's dead body forever ago, and also like it was yesterday. Housekeeping was here. They made the bed, cleaned the washrooms, fluffed the sofa cushions, and opened the curtains. There's no room service cart. There's no sign that someone died here. You'd never guess a murder happened here, or this room was the epicentre of a murder investigation.

When the porter knocks on the door, I open it. He props the door open and wheels the luggage cart inside.

"Would you mind waiting in the hall?" Emmy asks. "We'll bring the luggage to you in the hall."

"Sure," he says. "Whatever you like. Shout if you need me."

The porter wheels the cart back into the hall and stands next to it.

"Thank you," I say to him and smile.

"I don't want anyone else in here," Emmy says.

In silence, we collect Emmy's things, stuff them in random bags, zip up each bag as it becomes full, and take them to the porter in the hallway. He arranges the bags on the cart like he's playing an oversize game of Jenga.

"Just one more minute." I hand the last overnight bag to the porter, then return to the room and find Emmy. "That's it," I say. "Everything is on the luggage cart."

Emmy nods and sits on the edge of the bed.

"Do you want a few minutes alone?"

Emmy nods.

"I'll be in the hall." I pick up the keycard from the dresser. "I'm taking the keycard."

I close the door behind me and join the porter in the hall. We make small talk. He avoided the gut rot and says the scourge seems to be over because no one—except Gary—called in sick today. We run out of things to talk about and wait in bored silence until Emmy leaves the room.

"Ready?"

"Ready."

We turn toward the elevator and a door at the other end of the hall opens. Brad Hendricks and Sonia Chang emerge from the room. Together. They look at us and freeze like we caught them with their pants down.

"You have got to be kidding me," Emmy whispers when she sees her two biggest haters.

We exchange awkward waves with the unlikely couple.

"Did you like your flowers, Sonia?" I call down the hall. "Brad has great taste in florists, eh?"

I smile and give Brad a nod.

They stand glued to their spots by the door to Brad's room while Emmy and I follow the porter and the luggage cart onto the elevator.

"Flowers?" Emmy asks when the elevator door closes. I tell her about my conversations yesterday with Phillip and Brad. "Poppy didn't tell you Brad and Sonia were a couple?"

"I devote as little time and energy as possible to Brad and Sonia," Emmy says, dismissing them. "They're a perfect match. I hope they make each other miserable."

THE PORTER LOADS the luggage into my compact SUV, and Emmy follows me home in her rental car, which had been at the hotel since she joined Armando there on Saturday.

One by one, Emmy and I remove the bags from my

car and carry them into the house with Sophie following us back and forth.

As I reach into the car for another suitcase, Sophie barks and snarls, causing me to bolt upright and search for the source of her warning.

"What do you want?" I ask. "How do you know where I live?"

"You're on the Hendrick's Agency Christmas card list," Brad replies.

"I'd like you to remove me from your Christmas card list," I say, crossing my arms in front of my chest.

"Can I come inside and talk to you for a minute?"

"No. You can talk on the driveway."

"Ugh!" Emmy groans as she appears behind me. "What do you want, Brad?" She lets the screen door close behind her.

"Hi, Emmy," Brad says. "Listen, I owe you an apology. I'm sorry I accused you of murdering Armando, and for the other things I said to you on Sunday. Armando would've killed me for talking to you like that. I'm sorry."

"You knew, didn't you?" Emmy asks, ramming her hands into her hips.

"Knew what?" Brad asks.

"You knew Armando was a bigamist." She shifts her weight and leans toward him menacingly. "Didn't you?!"

"It's not that simple, Emmy," Brad replies as Emmy's frustrated moan drowns out the end of his sentence. "Armando was a complicated guy. But he loved you. He told me you're the only woman he ever loved."

This is the nicest thing I've heard Brad say. Ever. And he sounds sincere.

"Is that what you came to say?" Emmy asks. "You said it. You can leave now."

"I need to talk to Megan about something," he says.

Emmy marches to the car and wrestles a rolling suitcase out of the back seat.

"I'll be in the house," she announces, marching to the door. "Call me when *he's* gone, and I'll come back."

Emmy opens the door, follows the corgi into the house, and slams the door behind her.

"What do you want, Brad?"

"I want to apologize for yesterday."

"You'll have to be more specific."

"I'm sorry if my joke made you uncomfortable. I was kidding, but maybe I took it too far."

I assume he's referring to his offer to get together, but I feign ignorance.

"Are you referring to the lie you told me?"

"I didn't lie to you."

"Yes, you did."

"No, I didn't."

"You just did it again."

"Did what?" He laughs.

"Lied to me."

"What did I lie about?"

"You told me you bought flowers for your client who had a baby. I know for a fact they were for Sonia Chang."

217

"I was protecting my privacy." He shrugs. "It wasn't a lie."

"It wasn't the truth." I mimic his shrug. "Anyway, I heard Sonia dumped you. Why was she in your hotel room this morning?"

"Where do you get your information?" Brad chuckles and shakes his head. "What can I say? Sonia can't help herself." He smacks his hands against his broad chest. "Women get weak in my presence. Weak in the knees." He winks. "Are you feeling weak, Megan?"

"The only part of me that feels weak in your presence is my stomach. You make me sick," I scoff. "Why do you do that?"

"Do what?"

"As soon as you show a glimpse of humanity, you erase it by regressing into a narcissistic, predatory creep."

"Fine," Brad concedes. "I lied about the flowers. Sonia and I dated for a while, but she dumped me. She said the same thing as you. She said I have the emotional maturity of a carrot, and she can't be with someone who won't let themselves be vulnerable."

"Wow. Sonia and I agree on something," I sneer. "What about the message you sent with the flowers? What did, *do you regret it yet* mean? What would Sonia regret?"

"Dumping me," Brad replies like it's the only obvious answer. "I told her she'd regret it. She says she doesn't, but her visit to my hotel room this morning says otherwise, am I right?"

"If you say so." I sigh and roll my eyes.

"I want you to know I'm not Sonia's source. I didn't tell her anything about Armando's past, and I didn't confirm anything when she asked me. It's possible she gleaned something vague from overhearing my half of conversations with Armando, but whatever information she told you about him, she uncovered without my help."

"She didn't coax Armando's secrets from you during pillow talk?" I suggest.

"No. I'd never betray my best friend like that," Brad insists. "The flowers were the only thing I lied about yesterday, I swear. Everything else I said was true."

"I don't know if I believe you," I admit. "You're an effortless liar."

"Why would I lie about my best friend ignoring me? Why would I lie about walking away from his room when staying might have saved his life?"

"Because it's better than admitting you killed him?"

"You think *I* killed Armando?" Brad shouts, then looks around to make sure no one overheard him. "Why would I kill my best friend?"

"Because Armando was planning to fire you and sign with a new agent," I reply. "Your reputation for never being fired, and your bank account, would take a hit."

"Armando would never fire me," Brad says with confidence. "Trust me."

"He told Emmy he would."

"He said that to keep her sweet," Brad says. "Look, Armando was at the end of his career. He had one, maybe two seasons left, tops. It wouldn't be worth his while to fire me and sign with someone else. He'd have to pay me a lot of money to break his contract, and most agents don't want a client that close to retirement. Also, I was Armando's best friend. I know his secrets. He trusted me. He needed me."

What Brad says makes sense. On Friday, Armando said he was at the end of his career and wanted to go out on top.

"Secretsss?" I ask. "Plural? Armando had more secrets? Are his other secrets related to the bigamy?"

Does Brad know if Armando had children? Does he know the truth about the birth certificates Adam uncovered?

"I shouldn't have said anything," Brad says.

"Emmy has a right to know," I protest. "Did Armando keep other secrets from her?"

"I can't... Look... Armando..." He sighs. "I can't say anything else until I talk to my lawyer."

"Armando is dead. Who are you trying to protect?"

I'm confident the only person Brad wants to protect, ever, is himself.

"I'll say this." Brad takes a deep breath and lets it out. "Armando wasn't the soccer player everyone thought he was."

"What did he want?" Emmy asks after Brad leaves.

"I'm not sure, to be honest." I collapse on the living room sofa. Sophie jumps on the chair next to me and monitors the front yard through the window. "He apologized for being a jerk yesterday, then he was a jerk again. He admitted he and Sonia are in a situationship. He swears he didn't tell Sonia about Armando's first wife, but won't admit he knew Armando was a bigamist. He insists he didn't kill Armando."

"Of course, he does," Emmy replies. "Since Eric eliminated me as a suspect, Brad knows the police are closing in on him, and he's scared. Do you believe him?"

"Which part?"

Emmy shrugs. "Any of it?"

"I don't know," I admit. "Brad's a convincing liar. He clearly knows more than he admits. I get the sense he wants to talk, but his loyalty to Armando is stronger than his desire to unburden himself and do the right thing."

"My makeup bag and the bag with my electronics are still in the car. I'm going to get them. I'll be right back," Emmy says, slipping her feet into her shoes.

She disappears through the front door. I take a deep breath and contemplate what Brad said and didn't say, yesterday and today. I'm trying to find order in the chaos when Emmy comes back inside.

"They aren't there!" She throws her hands in frustration.

"Your makeup bag and electronics aren't in the car?" Emmy nods. "I remember you saying, *I'm taking my makeup bag and electronics to the porter.*"

Emmy nods. "Right after I said that, I saw my phone charger next to the bed. I put the bags on the washroom counter and left them there."

"It's understandable," I say. "You had a lot on your mind. I bet they're still where you left them."

"I'll ask Poppy to pick them up for me," Emmy says, reaching for her phone.

"We're taking a break from Poppy today, remember? It was your idea," I remind her. "I'm not ready to see her yet. I'll pick up your stuff."

"I'll come with you," Emmy says.

CHAPTER 25

ON THE DRIVE TO RISE & Glide, Emmy admits she suspected Poppy was the mystery blogger.

"I don't make Poppy's life easy, Sis."

"That doesn't give her the right to libel you," I say. "Poppy needs to find a healthier way to cope with her frustrations."

"We have a complicated relationship," Emmy says. "Our boundaries are blurrier than a foggy night."

"Just give me one day to be mad at her. You can resume normal dysfunction tomorrow."

My phone rings through the Bluetooth speaker of the car, and Eric's name and photo flash across the screen on the dashboard.

"Hey, handsome!"

"Hey, handsome!" Emmy echoes beside me.

"Hey, babe. Hey, Emmy. How's everyone's day?"

"OK." I pause. "Brad just left."

"Hendricks?"

"Uh-huh."

"He was in our house?"

"I sent him away, but Megan let him stay," Emmy interjects.

"No. We talked on the driveway."

"What did he want?"

"He apologized to Emmy, he apologized to me, then he befuddled me with doublespeak."

"The nerve of that guy showing up at the house! I'm meeting with him and his lawyer today. I'll warn him never to get within a hundred feet of you again. Hopefully, he'll recognize the person who delivered the drugged food to Armando and pick them out of a photo lineup."

"He knew about the bigamy."

"Did he admit he knew?"

"He wouldn't say he didn't know."

"He knew," Emmy adds.

"We just missed each other at Rise & Glide this morning. Did you get Emmy's stuff?"

"We did. It's all good. How are the interviews going?"

"Good. The only person missing from the employee list is Tina. Deb says Tina probably forgot to punch in. I'm at the office now, but as soon as Deb sends me copies of Tina and Gary's personnel files, I'll question Gary at his house, then head back to Rise & Glide to question Tina. She hadn't arrived for work yet when I left."

"Oh," I say, concerned about Eric picking up the gut rot virus at Gary's house and bringing it home. "Please be careful. Keep your distance and touch nothing."

WHEN WE PULL into the hotel parking lot, Rich Kendall, Sonia Chang, and other *Hello, today!* crew members are getting out of their cars.

"Do you mind if I pop over and compliment them on today's show?" Emmy asks.

"Take your time," I reply. "I'll call April back."

Emmy bolts out of the car to talk to her co-workers, and I call April and catch her up on everything that happened since we spoke yesterday. Our conversation is shorter than normal, because April has a lunch date with her parents, but she assures me she's keeping a close eye on the gossip blog, and there are no new posts.

I get out of the car to join Emmy, and the thud of the car door closing gets Rich Kendall's attention. He looks at me and waves with a smile.

"Hi, Rich." I wave.

He jogs over to me.

"Hi, Megan." Rich beams. "How are you?"

"I'm OK," I reply. "Good show this morning. The on-location segments you're doing in nearby towns are great. It's nice to see you outside of the studio, wearing something other than a suit."

"We're enjoying them too," Rich replies. "And the ratings have increased every day this week, so the viewers agree. How's Emmy doing?" He jerks his head toward the group of co-workers Emmy is with. "She puts on such a brave face."

"Emmy is resilient," I say, neither confirming nor denying how Emmy is coping.

"If there's anything I can do, please ask, Megan. I'm always available, and I'd do anything for Emmy. Anything at all to ease her pain."

"It would ease Emmy's pain to know who killed Armando and see them behind bars," I say.

"I would help if I could. If only I knew for certain…"

Rich's voice trails off before he finishes his sentence.

"If only you knew what for certain?" I ask, sensing he wants to disclose something. "You don't have to be certain, Rich. The police will determine the certainty of whatever information you have."

"I don't have any information," Rich says, chuckling and shaking his head.

"Rich, did you kill Armando?"

"No!" he insists. He glances around to see who else might be in earshot of our conversation. "I would never"—he snaps—"I love Emmy! I would never hurt her."

"Even if it meant Armando would be out of Emmy's life?" I ask. "And you could step in to help her through her grief?"

"That's twisted!" Rich decries. "Yes, I love Emmy. But if I'm ever lucky enough that she might reciprocate those feelings, I want it to be genuine. I don't want her to love me because she's confused and lonely in the wake of her husband's death."

"That's good to hear," I respond. "Emmy values your friendship, and she needs her friends more than ever. If you have any insight or thoughts about who killed Armando and why, it would help Emmy deal with his death and move on."

"I didn't kill Armando," Rich says with a sigh. "But I'm afraid if it weren't for me, he might still be alive."

"What do you mean?"

"I think I might have brought Armando's killer to Harmony Lake with me."

"Didn't you travel to Harmony Lake with Sonia Chang?" I ask, trying to recall the order in which the caravan of travelers arrived.

"Yes," Rich confirms. "Sonia is ambitious. When she wants something, she pursues it with relentless persistence."

"Do you think she's ambitious enough to commit murder?" I whisper.

"She can be frightening when she wants something." Rich nods.

"Why would Sonia kill Armando?"

"Sonia still has feelings for me," Rich explains. "She's jealous of the close friendship and working relationship Emmy and I share." He smiles. "Admit it, Emmy and I have great on-screen chemistry."

He clears his throat. "Also, Sonia and Emmy were both short-listed for the co-host job on *Hello today!*, but the network offered it to Emmy. Sonia's not used to losing. She never got over it. I'm afraid Sonia sees Emmy as the obstacle between her and her dream man and dream job."

"Wouldn't it make more sense for Sonia to kill Emmy instead of Armando?" I argue. "Emmy's death would leave an empty spot in your heart and on the *Hello, today!* sofa."

"I suspect Armando was collateral damage," he suggests. "When Sonia and I checked into the hotel, we saw your fiancé helping Emmy carry her luggage. They didn't see us."

"You and Sonia knew Emmy was in Armando's room the night before he died," I conclude.

Rich nods. "And I wonder if Sonia poisoned the wrong person's food."

Rich might be onto something. Through Brad, Sonia could find out Armando's room number. And if Brad told her he was planning to go to the gym with Armando on Sunday morning, she might have assumed Emmy was in the room alone, and the room service delivery was for her.

"Just let me grab my purse, and we can go inside," Emmy shouts, approaching the passenger side of the car.

Rich says a hasty goodbye, then jogs to catch up to his co-workers at the front door of the hotel.

Emmy opens the back door, slings her designer purse over her shoulder, and holds up a small wallet.

"I found this on the floor in the back seat," she says, handing me a red, faux-leather, compact wallet.

It has the same dimensions as a credit card, but fatter. I unzip the wraparound zipper and the wallet opens like an accordion, revealing about a dozen credit card slots. There's nowhere to keep coins or bills.

"Is it yours?" I ask.

Emmy shakes her head.

"Then whose is it? It's not mine."

I wrack my brain trying to remember who, aside from Emmy, was in my car and might've dropped their wallet. Deb Kee comes out of the hotel, intercepting us just as we reach the door. I zip the wallet shut and clutch it in my hand.

"You're back," Deb says with a smile. "What can I do for you?"

"I left two bags and a charging cord in room 814," Emmy explains. "My brain is a sieve right now," she chuckles. "May I get them?"

"Of course," Deb says. "If you'd like, someone can retrieve them, and you can relax in the lounge."

"Thank you, Deb, but I'd rather get them myself." Emmy says. "I'm worried I left something else behind, and I haven't realized it's missing yet. Checking the room once more will ease my mind."

"You'll need a keycard." Deb raises her index finger. "I'll be right back."

Deb disappears, then reappears minutes later, and hands Emmy a keycard.

On the elevator, I unzip the mystery wallet again. It's familiar. I've seen it before, but I can't place it. No one aside from Emmy has been in my car for days. Whoever owns the wallet is probably searching for it high and low, or they've already gone through the hassle of cancelling all their cards.

"Pull out a card." Emmy waggles her eyebrows at the wallet.

I slide a random card out of a slot. It's the back of a driver's license. I turn it over, and the photo that fills the left side of the card draws my focus. Emmy inspects the driver's license over my shoulder.

"Tina!" I say, looking at her photo and wondering how her driver's license ended up in my backseat. Then it hits me. "It must have fallen out of her jacket in my backseat this morning. I'll text her and let her know I have it."

I slide Tina's driver's license back into its slot.

"Read the name!" Emmy's voice is quick, and she struggles to swallow like she has a lump in her throat.

"What's wrong?" I ask.

Emmy's eyes are full of panic; her breaths are shallow and fast.

I flip the card over and read the name on Tina's driver's license.

Cristina Garcia Duran.

My heart pounds in my ears and my throat. I blink and read the name again, to be sure.

Emmy and I lock eyes.

Tina Duran, the knitter, is Cristina Garcia Duran, Armando's sister?

CHAPTER 26

THE ELEVATOR DOOR OPENS, but Emmy doesn't move. She's frozen. I grab her arm and yank her off the elevator. We hook arms and race-walk to room 814.

"Maybe Cristina Garcia Duran is a common name," I suggest when we're alone inside the room.

"This isn't a coincidence," Emmy says, shaking her head.

We sit on the sofa and, one by one, remove each card from the wallet and read the name. They all say Cristina Duran except for her government issued ID, which says Cristina Garcia Duran.

"What's this?" Emmy asks, unfolding a receipt that's wrapped around a card. "A receipt from a pharmacy in Harmony Hills." She hands it to me.

"It's a receipt for syrup of ipecac." I look at Emmy. "Why would Tina buy syrup of ipecac?"

"Megan!" Emmy slaps her hand across her mouth and tears fill her eyes. "Armando choked on vomit!

What if he threw up because Tina gave him syrup of ipecac?"

"The coroner's report didn't mention syrup of ipecac," I respond. "If Tina is Armando's sister, why didn't she tell us when she met you on Friday?"

"Did she know I was your sister before Friday?" Emmy asks.

"I didn't tell her, but someone else could have," I reply. "Even if Tina knew we're sisters, she couldn't have known you'd show up in Harmony Lake on Friday. No one knew until you got here."

"But it's a logical assumption that I'd show up eventually," Emmy reasons. "It's also a logical assumption that my husband would accompany me." She pauses and collects her thoughts. "I mention you on the show sometimes. I never use your name or mention Harmony Lake, but maybe over the years I gave away enough non-identifying information for Tina to find you."

"You think Tina moved to Harmony Lake and learned to knit so she could befriend me and lie in wait for you to bring Armando here?"

It's too far-fetched to be true, right? It's preposterous… isn't it?

"What other explanation is there?" Emmy asks. "What's the date on the receipt?"

I scan the bottom of the receipt.

"Friday October 1st. Just after 8 p.m."

"The day I arrived."

"And a few hours after Armando checked into the hotel where Tina works."

"I didn't realize she works here," Emmy says, shaking her head. "The Tina I met at Knitorious on Friday is the same Tina you and Eric were talking about on the phone, and the same Tina whose jacket you gave to Deb this morning."

"The same person." I nod. "I know her as Tina Duran. She's recently divorced and came to Harmony Lake to build a new life."

"And take care of some unfinished business."

"Who said that?" Emmy demands.

"Tina?" I say, stunned when, out of nowhere, she appears in the bedroom doorway.

"I overheard Emmy ask Deb if she could come up to the room," Tina explains. "I sneaked in and waited for you. I couldn't believe my eyes when I walked into Knitorious on Friday and you were standing behind the counter, Emmy. I'd waited so long for that moment. Then, your husband checked into the hotel where I work. It was too perfect. I couldn't have planned it better. I even borrowed a keycard from housekeeping and also sneaked in on Saturday morning to be sure it was him."

"You're Armando's sister?" Emmy asks, inspecting Tina with narrowed eyes.

I'm inspecting Tina too. Looking for a family resemblance between her and Armando. There's none.

"Armando Garcia is my brother," Tina confirms.

"Why did you kill your brother?" I ask.

"My brother isn't dead," Tina corrects me. "My brother, Armando Garcia, is alive and well in Ecuador.

He lives with his wife and their three children. He works as a bus driver. Armando has a happy life."

My phone rings and Eric's name and photo flash across the screen.

"I should answer it," I say. "If I don't, he'll worry. And he knows where we are."

"If you want to know why I killed your husband, don't let Megan answer," Tina says to Emmy, then she opens her mouth to reveal a lozenge clenched between her front teeth. "It's a fentanyl lozenge. I just took two Rohypnol tablets. I only have about fifteen minutes left."

"Spit it out!" I beg, as my phone stops ringing and Emmy's phone rings.

"Uh-uh," Tina says. "I didn't mean to kill him. His death was an accident. I can't live with myself, and I'm going to die the same way he did."

Emmy declines Eric's call, and moments later, we both receive a text message from him.

Eric: Tina delivered the food. She might be Armando's sister. Trying to locate her. Are you safe?

"I'll reply to Eric's text and throw him off your scent," Emmy says to Tina as her thumbs fly back and forth across her phone screen.

"If you didn't mean to kill him, why did you give him a lethal cocktail of drugs?" I ask.

"He should've passed out. I was going to take inappropriate photos of him, use the photos to blackmail him, then sell them to the media and ruin his life," Tina explains.

"You were going to take inappropriate photos of

your brother?" Emmy asks, placing her phone face down on the table in front of her. "Ewww."

My phone dings with the text reply Emmy sent to Eric and I.

Emmy: We're safe. Room 814. Don't come in until we shout for you. Bring Naloxone and an ambulance.

"I told you," Tina says, leaning against the door frame, "he wasn't my brother."

"Was the man you killed Mateo Cruz?" I ask? "Armando's best friend?"

"Former best friend," Tina corrects me. "How did you know?"

"I suspected, but I didn't know," I admit. "When Adam verified Sonia's claim that Armando was married, he also uncovered birth certificates for Armando's children. But Armando hasn't been to Ecuador since he signed his major league contract. He also found the legal guardianship papers showing that your parents became Mateo's legal guardians after Mateo's parents died, but he didn't find any trace of Mateo after that. Then, Armando's medical history included a broken collarbone, and a broken wrist. Both around the same age.

"Mateo was the sole survivor of a fatal car accident that killed his parents. When the coroner estimated the injuries occurred together, I wondered if they were from the accident. Armando made up stories to explain the healed fractures because he knew they might show up on CT scans or MRIs, and the team doctors would ask about them. And earlier today, Brad made a cryptic comment about Armando not being the soccer player everyone thought he was."

"You're good," Tina chortles.

Are her eyes getting heavy, or am I imagining it?

"I was married to Mateo Cruz?" Emmy asks. "Why did he use your brother's name?"

"He had no choice," Tina says. "It was a big mess, but Mateo used it to his advantage. Armando and Mateo were best friends and teammates. They played the same position. Years ago, their team travelled to a tournament, and when they arrived at their destination, the equipment manager realized some bags didn't make it onto the team bus. Almost half the team didn't have uniforms. Armando couldn't play in the tournament, but he went with them to cheer them on."

"Why couldn't Armando play?" Emmy asks.

"He had to rest his knee for a few weeks."

"Our-Armando told Emmy that Mateo suffered a career-ending knee injury," I say. "But it was your-Armando who injured his knee?"

"Yes," Tina confirms. "My brother Armando, the one who's alive and well, had a knee infection, and the doctor drained fluid that accumulated. It was not a career-ending injury. He was good as new after four weeks of rest. Mateo, the man I killed and who you knew as Armando, never injured his knee."

"What happened next?" Emmy asks.

"Soccer has pretty strict rules. Every player has to wear a uniform, *their own* uniform. The team couldn't get the missing uniforms in time, so they played with fewer players than normal. With fewer players to substitute, it was going to be a tough tournament."

"Did they have to forfeit the tournament?" I ask.

"That wasn't an option. The team would have to pay a fine, and the spectators would demand refunds. They had to play. Even though he couldn't play, Armando's jersey was among the ones that made it onto the bus. The coach and the team manager decided Mateo would wear Armando's uniform and play as Armando. They were similar height and had similar hair colours, and they were out of town where fewer people would recognize them. Unbeknownst to anyone, major league scouts were in the stands."

"The scouts thought they were watching Armando Garcia play soccer, but they were watching Mateo Cruz play soccer in Armando's jersey," I surmise.

"Exactly." Tina disappears into the bedroom and returns to the doorway seconds later with the chair from the desk. She sits down and fights a yawn. "The scouts were so impressed that they offered Mateo, who they knew as Armando, a major league opportunity."

"Why didn't Armando tell the scouts that the player who impressed them was actually Mateo?" Emmy asks.

"It would have been an enormous scandal," Tina explains. "Mateo wasn't the only player the scouts signed at the tournament. A scandal like that would've put all the major league contracts from the tournament in jeopardy. It would have destroyed careers and teams."

The irony makes me shake my head. The infection and draining procedure on real-Armando's knee might have healed as good as new, but his knee still ended his career. If not for the infected knee, Armando would have worn his own jersey and played in that tournament.

"The people in charge convinced Mateo to go along with it and pretend to be Armando Garcia?" I ask.

"They convinced both Armando and Mateo. And Mateo promised to share his major league earnings with my brother. He promised to send half of his earnings to Armando."

"Did Mateo honour the agreement?" Emmy asks.

"Yes," Tina replies, slouching forward and propping up her head with her hand. "Until he met Brad."

"I knew Brad had to be involved," Emmy hisses. "What did he do?"

"When your-Armando signed with Brad, his income increased because he earned income from sponsorship deals. But he only sent home half of his soccer earnings. He kept the rest of the earnings for himself. He insisted he earned the sponsorship money on his own, so he should keep it. My family disagreed. We believed that the sponsorship money too was possible only because he was pretending to be Armando. The argument escalated and got ugly. We threatened to expose his true identity."

"Why didn't you expose the scheme?" I ask.

"Because we feared the other people affected might harm us. Brad travelled to visit my family. He told the local government about our threat. Soccer is important to the local economy. The scandal would have destroyed so many people. They pressured my family to stay quiet. Brad offered my family a lump sum of money for signing something, promising never to disclose the scandal. The local officials pressured us to take it."

"You came to Harmony Lake, and bided your time, hoping Mateo-pretending-to-be-Armando would show up so you could blackmail him with dirty pictures, then sell the dirty pictures, and get the money you believe he owes your family," I surmise.

"I followed his soccer career like a rabid fan," Tina explains. "And when he married Emmy, I tuned into *Hello, today!* every day." She looks at Emmy. "Whenever you mentioned anything about your personal life, I wrote it down. Eventually, I pieced together that your sister lives in Harmony Lake and owns a business. My marriage was over. I had no reason to stay where I was, so I moved here. It didn't take long to find a recently engaged, forty-ish business owner whose daughter was away at university."

Tina looks at me. "I like you, Megan. You're my friend. You made me feel welcome, and you introduced me to other friends. I almost got cold feet and didn't go through with it. But I went through with it, and it went wrong. So wrong," Tina says, crying. "Instead of falling asleep, Mateo collapsed. I struggled to get him into bed, then he started twitching and shaking. He had a seizure or something. Brad sent a text, then showed up at the door, knocking and shouting. I watched through the peephole until Brad left, then I hung the DO NOT DISTURB sign on the door in case he came back, or someone else showed up. When I returned to his bedside, he was dead. I don't know what happened. I tried to make him look peaceful. Like he was sleeping."

"He threw up," I explain. "Armando's body tried to purge his stomach contents, but he was unconscious and on his back. He choked to death."

"Didn't Armando—I mean, Mateo—recognize you when he answered the door?" Emmy asks.

Tina shakes her head. "He had no clue who I was." She forces herself to sit upright and blinks rapidly a few times. "We hadn't seen each other in over twenty years. I've lived abroad most of that time. I look and sound different now."

Sensing that Tina is running out of time, I try to move her confession along.

"Deb said Gary delivered the food to Armando. How did you intercept him?"

"I almost didn't," Tina admits. "The kitchen is always busy. There was no opportunity to drug the food. When my co-workers started getting the stomach flu, it gave me an idea. I put ipecac in Gary's water bottle. He's one of those people who tracks his fluid intake every day. I knew it was his job to deliver Mateo's first meal on Sunday. I figured when the ipecac made him sick, everyone would assume he caught the stomach flu that's going around, and I would make sure I was nearby to take over Gary's duties. But Gary didn't get sick. Well not right away. I thought it didn't work, but I stayed close to him anyway, just in case. I waited in the service hall."

Tina jerks her thumb behind her, toward the door to the

service hall which is next door. "I was there when Megan picked you up for brunch. I knew Armando was alone in the room. Gary rolled the cart to room 814, then ran next door, and threw up all over the floor in the service hall. I reported Gary's illness to Deb, then took over his duties. I told Deb that Gary threw up *after* he delivered the food to room 814. I mixed the crushed-up drugs in Armando's food in the hallway, then knocked on the door. He wanted to eat in the bedroom, so I rolled the cart in there. Then I pretended to leave. But I didn't leave, I waited just inside the door. I ran in when I heard him collapse."

"You knew Gary would mention that he didn't finish the food delivery before he got sick, and that you were in the service hallway when he threw up, so you kept feeding him ipecac to prevent him from coming to work or answering questions for the police. You weren't taking soup to Gary because you're a kind person, you were lacing the soup with syrup of ipecac to keep him sick."

"He almost died too," Tina admits with silent tears streaming down her face. Her breaths are shallow and laboured. "That's when I knew I couldn't live with what I'd done. I knew I needed to confess and kill myself. I was going to write a letter, but I wanted to apologize in person." She looks at Emmy. "I'm so sorry, Emmy."

Tina collapses. Her head rolls back, forcing her jaw open, and her limp body slides out of the chair and onto the floor. Her head hits the wooden seat of the chair on her way down.

Is Tina breathing? Is she dead? Emmy grabs my hand and pulls me off the sofa.

"Now! Eric!" Emmy screams, clutching my hand and leaping over Tina's feet to get to the door.

Emmy opens the door, and we almost crash into two paramedics rushing to rescue Tina.

I resolve never to enter room 814 again.

CHAPTER 27

TUESDAY, October 19th

Eric sweeps into Knitorious and, with a victorious grin, slaps the list on the counter.

"That's it!" he declares, dusting his hands together. "Every Tupperware dish, casserole dish, and thank-you card, delivered."

"Thank you, honey." I kiss him, then he sinks into the sofa in the cozy sitting area, with a triumphant sigh and Sophie at his side.

We got home on Saturday from Armando's funeral. I continue to refer to him as Armando, because that's how we knew him.

But it took us until today to organize dishes, sign thank-you cards, and drop off everything to friends and neighbours.

The coroner released Armando's body the day after Tina's confession. Poppy helped Emmy arrange for a funeral home near Emmy to pick him up in Harmony

Lake and transport him. So far, the truth about Armando's identity, that he was Mateo Cruz pretending to be Armando Garcia, is still a secret. The real Garcia family doesn't want any negative attention from Tina's actions, so they allowed us to call him Armando at the service.

Emmy still feels violated by her husband's lie, but she's relieved he wasn't a bigamist, and that he truly loved her and only her. That being said, Emmy doesn't want to profit from Armando's death. She offered to give his estate to the real Garcia family, but they don't want it either. Together, Emmy and the Garcia family decided Armando's legacy will fund a soccer scholarship for underprivileged youth and provide soccer fields and equipment to underprivileged communities.

"Any update on Tina?" I ask, joining Eric on the sofa and picking up the Knitted Knocker I was working on before he arrived with his victory list.

On a positive note, The Charity Knitters are on track to have their most successful Knitted Knocker campaign ever. Thanks to Rich Kendall mentioning their campaign on *Hello, today!*, knitters from nearby towns have been making Knitted Knockers and dropping them off at Knitorious. There's a huge bin of them on the harvest table in the middle of the store.

"She's out of the hospital, and they transferred her to jail, but she's still under the care of a mental health team," Eric replies. "Tina knows Emmy recorded her confession, and she told her lawyer she'll plead guilty and accept the consequences of her actions."

Eric figured out Tina Duran and Cristina Garcia Duran were the same person when he received her personnel file from Deb. When he checked the employee list the night before, he looked for someone named Tina. He didn't know her last name, or that Tina is a short form of Cristina. Turns out she was on the list the entire time.

After Emmy texted Eric from the hotel room, to tell him not to come in until she shouted for him, she opened the voice recording app on her phone and recorded Tina's confession. Tina will face charges for Armando's murder and for poisoning her coworker. Gary has made a full physical recovery and returned to work at Rise & Glide.

"If only Brad Hendricks would accept—or even acknowledge—the consequences of his actions," I gripe.

Brad denies convincing the Garcia family to accept a lump sum payment and sign a nondisclosure agreement about Armando's true identity. Despite the police tracking down his travel history, and proving that he was near the Garcia family when they received their lump sum payment, Brad insists he was on vacation, and the timing was a coincidence. With no one willing to say otherwise, Brad won't face consequences for his part in perpetuating Armando's lie. The injustice infuriates me, but I believe what comes around goes around, and Brad will receive his comeuppance sooner or later.

"At least he cooperated with the murder investigation," Eric reminds me. "After Tina confessed, Brad picked her out of a photo lineup as the person he saw knocking on Armando's hotel room door the morning he died. Gary told us Tina was in the service hallway when he threw up, but he couldn't place her with Armando's food. Only Brad could do that."

"Good morning!" Connie sings as she breezes through the front door. "Did you watch *Hello, today!* this morning?"

Sophie leaps off the sofa to greet her.

"We did," I reply. "The show is even better with the new producer. And the on-the-road episodes are my favourite!"

Yesterday was Emmy's first day back at work since Armando died. While she was on bereavement leave, Sonia Chang resigned from the network, and the new producer hopes to capitalize on the success of the on-location episodes in Harmony Lake by taking the show on location one week per month. To start, they're visiting hometowns of the cast and crew.

"Mine too!" Connie agrees. "This week they're visiting Rich Kendall's hometown, and it looks like such a cozy, sweet community. And the atmosphere on the show is much more relaxed without Sonia. The banter between Rich and Emmy is even more entertaining than usual."

While Tina was confessing to Emmy and I in room 814, Sonia Chang was emailing the head honcho of the network. She tendered her resignation, effective that day. Less than forty-eight hours later, she sat in the anchor seat at a rival network and aired an in-depth exposé about corruption in reality television. She specifically unveiled behind-the-scenes corruption at *Perfect Match*. According to Sonia Chang, and the proof she uncovered, the outcome of *Perfect Match* was predetermined, and viewer votes were meaningless.

To say April was upset is an understatement. Her favourite reality TV show was fake. She swears she'll never trust reality TV again.

The network paid contestants hush money to follow a script and keep quiet about the predetermined outcome. As a result, *Perfect Match* was cancelled, several people associated with the show lost their jobs, and the previous seasons' celebrity contestants lost a lot of angry fans. Some even lost their jobs on other shows.

I have a theory about Sonia Chang's investigation into *Perfect Match*. I suspect Sonia discovered the corruption at *Perfect Match* from her friend, who is a producer on the show. She recommended Emmy and Armando as contestants on the next season of *Perfect Match*, so they would be in the crossfire when the show imploded because of her exposé. To increase the impact of her comeback story, she would've exposed Armando's alleged bigamy. Little did Sonia know, if she'd kept digging when she found the real Mrs. Garcia, she would've exposed an even bigger case of corruption: Armando's true identity. Emmy and Armando's marriage probably wouldn't have survived the public probing, and Emmy would've lost her job and reputation for sure. Sonia would've gotten revenge against Emmy for taking the job on *Hello, today!* and Rich Kendall's heart, and Sonia would've re-established herself as the queen of investigative reporting. Armando's murder thwarted Sonia's plan. She jumped ship to another network and aired her investigative report sooner than planned.

"Did you guys read Poppy's new blog post?" April asks, her voice competing with the jingle of the bell over the door.

Her abrupt entrance startles Sophie, who jumps to attention.

"No," I reply, my heart sinking into my stomach. "Is it another anti-Emmy post?"

So far, Poppy has remained true to her word and hasn't posted anymore anti-Emmy blog posts since I confronted her about being the mystery blogger. Emmy and Poppy talked it out, and Poppy admitted that being Emmy's best friend and assistant was too much. Poppy resigned as Emmy's assistant but kept her status as Emmy's best friend. In fact, Poppy had to hire an assistant for herself after her recent overnight success.

Following the *Perfect Match* fiasco, Poppy's little-known, anonymous gossip blog got a lot of attention from readers who found it while searching online for information about *Perfect Match* and the show's previous contestants. The blog became so popular so fast that Poppy now runs it full time. She sells advertising space for obscene amounts of money, and instead of relying on her invisibility superpower to learn tidbits of gossip about B- and C-list celebrities, she gets tips from all over the world about A-list celebrities. According to Poppy, the tipsters are often celebrities themselves, looking for publicity or trying to control how they're portrayed in the media.

"I think Poppy is too busy to post about Emmy,"

April teases. "But listen to this. *For Stitcher, For Poorer, In Stitchness and in Health.* I think the headline is a nod to you Megnificent." April clears her throat and continues,

"*Wedding bells will ring this Christmas for a certain A-list celebrity actor, who's returning to the scene of the crime to put a ring on it. The alliterative actor will say her vows surrounded by love and harmony. Lake on one side and mountains on the other, the celebrity couple booked every room, cabin, and cottage in between, so their nuptials will be cozy and paparazzi-free.*"

"Someone is getting married?" I venture a guess. "Someone who's first and last initials are the same... someone who visited Harmony Lake before..."

"It's Jules Janssen!" April blurts out before she explodes from waiting for me to piece it together.

"Jules Janssen is getting married in Harmony Lake?" I ask. "To whom?"

"The co-star she fell in love with. You know, that handsome guy. The tall one?" April raises her hand above her head to show me what tall means. "He's handsome and sultry. He has that hair." She musses the top of her long blonde hair, then pushes my shoulder. "You know who I mean."

I don't know who she means.

"Oh! *Him!*" Connie agrees, snapping her fingers and nodding. "I know who you mean. He has that voice and does the thing with his eyebrows." She does a weird thing with her eyebrows.

"Yes!" April points at Connie. "Him. He's the guy Jules Janssen is marrying in Harmony Lake at Christmastime."

"It's just a rumour," I point out. "It's a gossip blog. And Poppy didn't mention any names."

"When is Poppy's blog ever wrong?" April challenges.

"She's right, my dear," Connie agrees. "Poppy's blog hasn't been wrong yet."

"Think about all the A-list celebrities walking up and down Water Street, in and out of our stores," April remarks, absorbed in the fantasy.

My phone and April's phone chime in unison. It's a text from the WSBA—the Water Street Business Association.

"See, I told you it's true," April says smugly, then shows Connie the text.

"What?" Eric asks.

"Jules Janssen just booked every room at Rise & Glide, King of the Hill, and the Hav-a-nap motel," I reply.

"I'm surprised she wants to come back here," Eric comments.

"Jules said Harmony Lake was beautiful," I recall out loud. "She even talked to Adam about filming here."

"Last time she came to town, she ended up in the middle of a murder investigation," Eric says. "Why would she want to get married in a town where she was once a murder suspect?"

"There's no such thing as bad publicity?" Connie suggests with a shrug.

"I'm sure it'll be fine," April retorts. "People don't die at weddings."

I hope not.

KEEP READING for a sneak peek of In Stitchness and in Health: A Knitorious Murder Mystery Book 10.

CLICK HERE to read an exclusive Life Crafter Death bonus scene.

IN STITCHNESS AND IN HEALTH

CHAPTER 1

Thursday December 16th

There's a low-key hum of restless energy running through Harmony Lake. It vibrates through me the same way an approaching train does moments before it's visible from the station platform.

On the outside Harmony Lake is a life-sized snow globe; a cozy, postcard-worthy winter wonderland. But on the inside, we're on the brink of chaos. Next week hundreds of A-list celebrities will descend on our sweet, snowy town. Hundreds of paparazzi from around the world will follow them, for what the media has dubbed, *the celebrity wedding of the century.*

World-famous actor Jules Janssen and her equally famous and beautiful fiancé have chosen Harmony Lake as the venue for their much-anticipated Christmas eve wedding. They've booked every hotel, motel, vacation rental, and bed-and-breakfast in town for the comfort of their VIP guests, and to prevent the parasitic paparazzi from finding local accommodation. They want to get married in peace. The love-struck couple wants a private, intimate affair with only several hundred of their nearest and dearest.

"Are you going to ask for autographs?" April asks, gazing into the distance and daydreaming about the celebrities who will venture into her bakery, Artsy Tartsy.

April is my best friend. We've known each other since I moved to Harmony Lake almost twenty years ago. We met at a mummy-and-me playgroup when our daughters were babies.

"I haven't thought about it," I reply.

"T says it's tacky to ask for autographs." April crosses her arms in front of her chest and huffs. "Like T wouldn't ask for an autograph if Oprah walked into our bakery. Or George Clooney," she adds under her breath.

T is April's wife. Her full name is Tamara, but everyone calls her T. She's Artsy Tartsy's talented pastry chef and she's less star-struck than April, which isn't saying much because most people are less star-struck than April. She's the most dedicated celebrity-watcher I know.

"It's too quiet," I comment. "I miss the pre-Christmas hustle and bustle. It's peaceful without any tourists, but it's also kind of eerie."

Harmony Lake is a tourist town. City escapees flock to our lake in the summer, and our mountains in the winter. This should be one of the busiest weeks of the year, but without tourists my yarn store, Knitorious, is dead. Local knitters have already purchased the yarn and supplies they need for Christmas knitting and now they're nestled snugly at home, knitting as fast as they can to beat the Christmas eve deadline.

"Enjoy the quiet while you can, it'll be plenty busy this weekend when the celebrities arrive!" April rubs her hands in front of her. "Imagine the rich and famous wandering in and out of Knitorious, asking you knitting questions and touching everything." Her blue eyes are bright and her voice is giddy, like a kid on Christmas morning.

"Easy for you to say," I say. "Artsy Tartsy is so busy baking for the wedding that you had to hire a second pastry chef to help. And everybody loves dessert, so the bakery will have lots of customers. I doubt our famous visitors will be as hungry for yarn and knitting supplies as for T's delicious desserts." I sigh. "This wedding will be a media circus. I can't wait until Harmony Lake goes back to normal."

"Knitorious has benefitted from the wedding too," April reminds me. "You said your online sales are way up over last December."

"They are," I admit. "And I'm grateful, but I still miss the in-person customers."

Online business is booming, thanks to the publicity from Jules Janssen's upcoming nuptials. Online orders are through the roof and Knitorious is trending toward having our best December in history. But I still miss the tourists. Other local businesses, like Artsy Tartsy, are busy preparing for the wedding. It's unfortunate for me that Jules Janssen's star-studded celebration doesn't require yarn or needlework supplies.

The tourists bring a certain energy with them though, and that energy is part of what makes Harmony Lake feel like home. We need the tourists, and they need us.

"Speaking of weddings," April says, crossing her arms in front of her chest and tilting her head so her long blonde ponytail swings like a pendulum. "Have you set a date yet?" She arches her eyebrows. "You've put off picking a date every month since you and Eric got engaged. What's the hold up?"

"We're working on it," I reply, trying not to smirk.

This might be another reason I don't share everyone's collective enthusiasm for Jules Janssen's wedding. It's a constant reminder that *I* need to plan a wedding.

I love Eric and I can't wait to marry him, but I'm not looking forward to planning the wedding. We've both been married before, and we've both done the big-wedding thing. Just thinking about all the planning, decisions, and details that are necessary to pull off even a simple wedding makes me want to elope. But eloping isn't an option, we already discussed it. We'd never stop hearing about it from our friends and family, and to be honest, I can't imagine getting married without them. We want everyone we love to be there. Since it's unlikely the universe will send us a Christmas miracle disguised as a fully planned wedding with all the details pre-arranged, I'll have to do it. And I will. Right after Christmas, I swear.

"What aren't you telling me?" April asks. "I know that smirk, Megnifico. You have a secret."

April likes to come up with nicknames that are based on my actual name, Megan. Today I'm Megnifico.

"We're getting married at the end of May," I admit, then point to April and give her a stern look. "Don't tell anyone. Nothing has been confirmed yet."

"May is nice," April contemplates, staring off into the distance. "Warm weather and long days."

"Hannah will be home for the summer," I add. "Harmony lake will be between tourist seasons, and it will give our families enough time to make travel arrangements."

Hannah is my daughter. She's in her third year of university in Toronto, but right now she's home for Christmas.

"Good morning, my dears," Connie sings, drowning out the jingle of the bell over the door. "This is from Eleanor Bigg." She drops a yellow paper gift bag on the counter on her way to the backroom to hang up her coat. "Scrap yarn for the yarn drive," she croons, her sing-song voice growing fainter as she gets closer to the back room.

"Thank you!" I call after her.

Startled by Connie's arrival, my dog, Sophie, jolts awake from her nap, jumps off the sofa in the cozy sitting area, and gives her short, corgi body a good shake. Then she trots after Connie toward the backroom.

"That reminds me," April says, nodding toward the paper bag on the counter. "I have some scrap yarn to donate, too. How long are you collecting it?"

"Until the end of the month."

The local charity knitting guild is collecting yarn. They're accepting donations of scrap yarn for an upcoming, top-secret, yarn bombing project.

Yarn bombing is to knitters and crocheters what graffiti is to street artists. But instead of spray paint or chalk, knitters and crocheters create colourful displays in yarn. They adorn lamp posts, bike racks, stop signs, statues, and anything else that stays put, with colourful knitted and crocheted fabric.

"I told Mrs. Bigg we would remember to enter her name in the draw," Connie announces upon her and Sophie's return from the backroom.

"Got it."

I write Mrs. Bigg's name on a ballot and poke it into the slot on top of the ballot box.

Knitorious is the collection hub for the yarn donation drive. To encourage donations, we're entering the donors into a draw to win a Knitorious gift card.

"Oooh, wait until you see the gorgeous scarf Mrs. Bigg is working on," Connie adds. "She was binding it off when I ran into her at the library. It's such a lovely yarn. She bought it when she and Mr. Bigg were on vacation last month. The scarf is for her son and she's making him a matching hat." Connie picks up the paper bag from the counter and opens it. "Maybe she put some of the leftover yarn in here," she says, shaking the bag and peering inside. She raises her reading glasses to her eyes from where they dangle around her neck like a necklace. "It's the loveliest shade of cerulean blue with beige tweed flecks. And so soft. It's a merino-camel hair blend." She folds the bag shut, reseals the decorative tape, and abandons it on the counter. "There's none in here." She smiles, tucking a chunk of her sleek, silver, chin-length bob behind her ear.

Connie is one of the most beautiful, sophisticated women I know. I hope when I'm seventy years young, I age with just some of Connie's grace and style.

I take the paper bag to the back of the store and drop it in the donation box with the rest of the donated yarn, making a mental note to sort it by weight before the charity knitters pick it up at the end of the month.

"Megan and I were just discussing weddings," April declares, encouraging Connie to join her in peer-pressuring me to set the wedding wheels in motion. "What do you think about a May wedding, Connie?"

I asked April to keep quiet about our May wedding, but that vow of silence doesn't apply to Connie, and April knows it. April and Connie aren't just my friends. They're family. We're a non-traditional family of choice.

"A May wedding will be lovely," Connie says, smiling from ear to ear and bringing her hands together in front of her chin. "A spring wedding! I can't wait!"

Connie and April were the first friends I made in Harmony lake eighteen years ago. Connie is my mother-friend. She calls me her daughter-friend. My ex-husband and I moved here when Hannah was a baby. He was a workaholic, I was a new mum, and I was grieving because my mum passed away just before we moved here. I was lonely and overwhelmed. I grief-knitted during Hannah's naps and after her bedtime, until I ran out of yarn. Connie and I met when I pushed Hannah's stroller into Knitorious to replenish my yarn stash. Connie took Hannah and me under her wing and filled the mother and grandmother-shaped holes in our hearts. We became fast friends, and soon we were family. When Hannah was older, Connie hired me to work part time at Knitorious, and when she retired a couple of years ago, I took over the store. Now, I own Knitorious and Connie works here part time.

"Have you booked a venue?" Connie asks.

"We'd like something informal," I explain, hoping they don't realize that when I say *informal,* I mean simple and easy to plan. "We're thinking we might book the pub, or have an outdoor barbecue."

Their blank stares speak volumes. Connie and April are unimpressed. Even Sophie's glare is heavy with disappointment. They're looking forward to a bigger, more formal wedding with all the traditions and trimmings.

"The pub won't be big enough to hold everyone," Connie says, shaking her head and tucking a few more strands of sleek, silver hair behind her ear.

"And where would you have the barbecue?" April asks. "What if it rains? You'll need multiple, massive tents."

"April is right, my dear," Connie agrees. "You can't have hundreds of people huddled under a few tiny tents."

"Hundreds?" I ask, wondering if I even *know* hundreds of people.

"Who *won't* you invite, my dear?"

I open my mouth to answer, but I can't. Connie's right. Everyone in town will want to come, and Eric and I will want them there. It never occurred to me that, in a town as small as Harmony Lake, our wedding would be a public event. This is a hazard of living in a friendly, tight-knit community—hundreds of people love us and want to share in our special day.

Still speechless, I'm saved by the literal bell when the door swings open.

Chapter 2

"Megan Martel?" the courier asks, eyeing all three of us.

April and Connie point at me.

"That's me," I say.

"Sign here."

He hands me the stylus and I sign the screen.

"Can I leave it on the counter?" he asks, dropping the box on the counter without waiting for a reply.

He squats down to greet Sophie, rubbing her between the ears. He reaches into his pocket and looks up at me. I nod. He pulls out a dog treat and gives it to Sophie.

"Thank you," I say, smiling.

"Have a nice day." He smiles, stands up, then looks down at Sophie. "See you later, Sophie."

He leaves.

It's amazing that a courier who has made deliveries to Knitorious for years can be on a first name basis with my dog, yet when faced with three completely different looking women, has to ask which one is me.

"Is that your dress?" April asks.

I nod.

"The one you ordered for the police gala next month?" Connie asks.

I nod again.

Eric and I are attending a police gala next month. It's a black-tie event and we'll have to spend a night in the city. It's an award ceremony and fundraising event. Eric will receive an award for his perfect murder-solving record.

"I love this dress," I say, running my hand along the taped seam of the box. "I fell in love with it the second I saw it. But the boutique only had my size in *Blood Rush Red*. They special-ordered it for me in *Midnight Rendezvous*."

I pluck the letter opener from the mug of pens next to the cash register, slice the packing tape, and fold back the box flaps. A sticker bearing the boutique's logo seals the blush-coloured tissue paper that envelops my dream dress. However, excitement turns to disappointment when I tear the sticker, part the tissue paper, and find myself staring at the wrong dress. I exhale a long, loud breath.

"What is it, my dear?" Connie asks, setting her knitting on the table and standing up.

"They sent me the wrong dress," I reply, pouting and lifting the white dress out of the box. "This isn't *Midnight Rendezvous*." I trap the dangling tag between my thumb and forefinger and read it aloud. "*Wife of the party.*" My shoulders slump. "What a lame name for a colour."

"It's a beautiful dress," April says.

"I'm sure the store can fix it," Connie suggests. "The gala isn't until next month. There's lots of time to exchange it for *Midnight Rendezvous*."

I sigh and lower the dress back into the box.

"The universe doesn't make mistakes, Megpie," April counsels. "Maybe instead of the dress you *want,* the universe sent you the dress you *need*."

"Why would I need a white dress for a black-tie function?" I ask.

"Everything happens for a reason." April shrugs. "Only the universe knows why."

"The universe can have whatever reasons it wants, but I don't have to agree."

"Try it on," urges Connie. "I'd like to see it on you. Even if it is, *Wife of the Party* instead of *Midnight Rendezvous*."

With no more coaxing, I retreat to the washroom to try on the dress.

"It's gorgeous!" I mutter to myself, looking in the full-length mirror on the washroom door.

Shades of white and off-white rarely flatter my pale skin, but somehow, this dress compliments my fair complexion. I take the hair tie from my wrist and grip it between my teeth. I twist my long, brown curls into a messy bun, ignoring the few rebellious tendrils that fall around my face. This dress definitely requires an updo. And neutral eye makeup on my hazel eyes. But a bold lipstick. Red. Yes! Cranberry or Holly. *Sigh.* "I wish I could get away with wearing a white dress to a black-tie event." *Sigh.*

"It's beautiful," April says when I emerge from the washroom.

"Breathtaking, my dear."

"Now that you're wearing it, it's more ivory than pure white," April observes. "The colour is gorgeous on you."

"I like it too."

I turn to show off the back of the dress.

The form-fitting bodice has an open back and a wide boat neck with short cap sleeves. A tea-length, full skirt flows out from the bottom of the fitted bodice. I swing my hips, and the skirt billows around my legs. This dress fits like it was custom made for me.

"It would be a lovely wedding dress," Connie points out.

I hate to dampen her enthusiasm, but this dress is too formal for the casual wedding Eric and I envision.

"We don't know for sure when or where we're getting married," I remind her. "If I didn't wear it as a wedding dress, when would I ever wear such a white, expensive dress?"

Disappointed to send it back to the store, I take off the dress, lovingly refold it, lay it in the box, and reseal it.

"*Hmmmph!*" I huff after I end the call. "The store won't pay the shipping cost to return the dress. And I won't pay the shipping cost because it would be much less expensive to make the two-and-a-half hour round trip and return the thing myself."

"But it's their fault. They sent you the wrong dress," April sympathizes.

"I know, but they made an exception by shipping it to me. They only offer in-store pickup. The store manager made an exception because I live far away. They won't pay to ship it twice." I shrug. "I understand their position, I just don't like it. The manager said I have thirty days to return it. I'll go after the holidays to avoid the Christmas rush."

"What will you wear to the gala?" Connie asks.

"I'll shop for something else when I return the dress, otherwise I have a few options in my closet. It was this specific dress." I tap on the box. "I fell in love with it."

The bell over the door jingles, and Sophie springs to attention, ready to greet the newcomer.

"Hey, handsome! I thought you had a big meeting this morning with Jules Janssen's security team?"

Eric kisses me on the forehead and hands me a to-go cup from Latte Da.

"They cancelled." He shrugs.

"Again? Did they reschedule?" I ask. "The VIPs fly in tomorrow."

"They didn't reschedule." He sits in one of the over-stuffed chairs with a sigh. "Fine with me. They asked for the meeting."

Sophie jumps up and nestles into his lap, and he scratches her neck.

Eric is the chief of the Harmony Lake Police Department. Jules Janssen's security team has been harassing him to meet with them about the security arrangements for the wedding. They want to coordinate efforts to protect the wedding guests and manage the unwanted media people. This is the third time they've cancelled, but it's the first time they haven't rescheduled.

While Eric talks to Connie and April, I crack the lid on my gingerbread latte and savour the moment when the warmth of the first sip touches my soul.

"Is that the dress you ordered for the gala?" Eric asks, nodding at the box on the counter.

"It's the dress I'm returning to the store."

"Where's the dress for the gala?"

"Either at the mall, or in my closet."

Eric furrows his brow. His brown eyes and handsome face cloud with confusion. But before I can elaborate, the bell jingles again. The only place busier than Knitorious today is Santa's workshop.

"Hi, Amber!" I smile.

Amber Windermere is Jules Janssen's executive project planner. Amber says it's a fancy title for an event planner. She's been staying in Harmony Lake since October, overseeing the seemingly endless wedding details.

"Hi, Megan." Amber smiles. "Hi everyone." She smiles and waves at everyone in the cozy sitting area.

Amber is young,—I'd guess mid-twenties—and ambitious. I've only known her for a couple of months, but she's career-focused, and determined to make this wedding an enormous success. According to Amber, if this wedding goes off without a hitch, it will launch her career to a whole new level. When I asked how she landed such a high-profile gig, Amber told me Jules requested her because she was so pleased with a previous party Amber organized for her.

"I have a donation for the yarn drive," Amber explains, reaching into her bag. "It looks like I'll be leaving town sooner than expected and I won't be needing this yarn."

I've been teaching Amber how to knit. Event planning is stressful,—especially when the entire world is watching—and she was looking for a hobby to help her relax. We knit together a few times each week. Amber is a brilliant student. She mastered the knit and purl stitches right away, and her stitches are remarkably consistent for someone who swears she's never picked up knitting needles before we met.

"Are you sure?" I ask. "You're doing so well. Maybe if your next wedding is stressful, you'll want to pick up the needles again."

"That's sweet of you to say, Megan." Amber says. "But you're the only person I know who knits. After I leave Harmony Lake, I won't have a knitting guru to help me."

I'm about to offer to video chat with Amber when she needs knitting help, and recommend several good YouTube channels for new knitters, but Connie speaks first.

"Why are you leaving town, Amber? Is everything alright? Is there a problem at home?"

"Nothing like that...." Amber says, flashing Connie a wide, bright, reassuring smile.

Amber opens her mouth to continue speaking, but doesn't get the chance because our local florist Phillip rushes in. His eyes search the store with determined urgency, until his focus lands on Amber.

"Is it true?" Phillip demands, glaring at her. "Is it true that Jules Janssen cancelled her wedding? She and her huge guest list aren't coming to Harmony Lake?"

The wheeze from our collective gasp could rival a giant air mattress with a leak.

Click here to read the rest of In Stitchness and in Health.

ALSO BY REAGAN DAVIS

Knit One Murder Two

Killer Cables

Murder & Merino

Twisted Stitches

Son of a Stitch

Crime Skein

Rest In Fleece

Life Crafter Death

In Stitchness and in Health

Bait & Stitch

Murder, It Seams

Neigbourhood Swatch: A Knitorious Cozy Mystery Short Story

Sign up for Reagan Davis' email list to be notified of new releases and special offers: www.ReaganDavis.com/email/email. Follow Reagan Davis on Amazon.

Follow Reagan Davis on Facebook, Bookbub, Goodreads, and Instagram

ABOUT THE AUTHOR

Reagan Davis is a pen name for the real author who lives in the suburbs of Toronto with her husband, two kids, and a menagerie of pets.

When she's not planning the perfect murder, she enjoys knitting, reading, eating too much chocolate, and drinking too much Diet Coke.

The author is an established knitwear designer who has contributed to many knitting books and magazines. I'd tell you her real name, but then I'd have to kill you. (Just kidding! Sort of.)

http://www.ReaganDavis.com/

Made in the USA
Columbia, SC
07 June 2023

17807945R00167